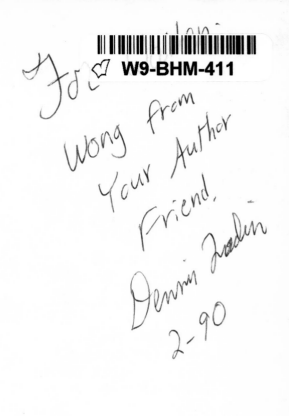

For [...]den:
Wong from
Your Author
Friend,
Dennis Fradin
2-90

HOW I SAVED THE WORLD

HOW I SAVED THE WORLD

by **Dennis Brindell Fradin**

GEMSTONE BOOKS

Dillon Press, Inc.   Minneapolis, Minnesota 55415

For my children—
Anthony, Diana, and Michael

Library of Congress Cataloging-in-Publication Data

Fradin, Dennis B.
  How I saved the world.

  "Gemstone books."
  Summary: After thirteen-year-old Shelley spots a UFO
one summer night at a rundown resort in northern Michigan,
he becomes involved in a desperate effort to stop an alien
invasion.
  [1. Science fiction]   I. Title.
PZ7.F8416Ho 1986   [Fic]   86-11585
ISBN 0-87518-355-7

Dillon Press, Inc., 242 Portland Avenue South
Minneapolis, Minnesota 55415

Printed in United States of America
1 2 3 4 5 6 7 8 9 10 95 94 93 92 91 90 89 88 87 86

Contents

1 We Go to the Country *1*

2 The Strange Blue Lights *14*

3 Trish Vincent *21*

4 The Flying Saucer Lands *33*

5 No One Believes Me *44*

6 Too Good To Be True *56*

7 Marsha Coe *71*

8 They're Aliens! *80*

9 The Alien in the Fifty-Dollar Jeans *88*

10 My Girl Friend, Trish *98*

11 A Close Call *109*

12 "Such Pleasant Folks" *119*

13 Last-Second Preparations *128*

14 The Weird Room *135*

15 We Humans Strike Back *150*

1

We Go to the Country

Entry from my diary of August 12, 1984:

Last night I went out to look at the stars with Uncle Myron. We looked through his telescope and we talked about galaxies and how big the universe is and stuff like that. We were lying on lawn chairs at about midnite when six blue lights floated over Indianface Mountain and headed toward us. When they passed overhead, we saw that they were on the bottom of a round space ship. It went over us spinning like a giant Frisbee and making a very soft whir-rr-rrr sound maybe 200 feet over our heads. We watched it float over the forest and then land three or four miles away, Uncle Myron figured. I wasn't scared when the space ship went over, but when I got into bed by myself I had these little shakes. All night I kept sitting up and looking outside my bedroom window because I was afraid creatures were outside staring in at me.

My freshman English teacher, Mr. Munk, taught us it's good to start with something exciting even in a nonfiction story, so I've copied my diary from August 12, 1984, to show how the whole business of my saving the world began. Mr. Munk also taught us that "background, buildup, and details make a story interesting." I'm sure that's doubly true when it comes to telling an important and true story, as I'm about to do. I mean, if I started right in on how I saved the world from the "people" on the UFO, would you believe me? So, thanks to good old Mr. Munk, I'm going to try to give my story the proper background, buildup, and details. It's a true (and sometimes sad) story that involves every one of you. Anyway, it *would* have involved you if I hadn't saved the world.

My story starts in late July of 1984 when the Monahans (my family) were in our old blue station wagon, Calamity, chugging north from Chicago to Upper Michigan. In case you don't know, Michigan is divided into two parts—the Upper and Lower peninsulas. If you look at a map, you'll find Upper Michigan right on top of Wisconsin.

"It's one of the least populated places in the United States," Dad said, flooring the accelerator on the highway approach. It didn't do much good because the wagon was loaded down with clothes, books, pots, a typewriter, and us four humans. "There's nothing but forests, mountains, lakes, and little towns up there," he added.

"You kids'll breathe fresh air and enjoy nature for a whole month!" Mom enthusiastically said. "And Uncle Myron'll show you the stars through his telescope."

2

Mom and Dad didn't see my little sister, Jane, and me making faces in the backseat. We'd have rather spent the summer with TV and pollution and our friends than with fresh air and stars and nothing to do.

Mom, who was sitting in the front seat next to Dad, had the map and a notebook on her lap. She was writing a poem in the notebook. Mom teaches English Literature at Eisenhower Junior College in Chicago, but what she really loves is to work on the book of poetry she's been trying to write ever since I can remember. In fact, she always keeps a piece of paper in her bra and a Bic pen in her frizzy hair in case she has an inspiration to write something. Many a time Mom has gone into the bathroom and come out an hour later with a notebookful of poems. And sometimes when she's making dinner, she'll get this far-off look in her eyes and write a poem right there at the kitchen counter. If dinner burns she'll say something like "Oh, what kind of mother am I?" Jane and I always reply that she's a great mother (it's true) and that we know she has to write when she's inspired. Don't think we're so nice. Burned dinner means McDonald's or Kentucky Fried, which are better than Mom's meat loaves and cheese casseroles anyway.

Dad, who teaches Latin and Greek Literature at Stevenson College on Chicago's North Side, is pretty strange, too. Dad's a scholar, meaning he'd rather read a book or go to a museum than watch the World Series on TV. For the past few years he's been writing a book called *Virgil for Kids*, which he thinks is going to be a big hit with high school Latin teachers across the nation. Dad's convinced that just

3

about all the things people are interested in today are just fads. "Virgil and Catullus will be read long after people have lost interest in computers and video games" is one of Dad's pet sayings.

The main reason we were heading up to the country was so that Mom and Dad could work on their books in peace and quiet. We were going to stay for a month at Uncle Myron's resort in an old, abandoned copper-mining town called Copper Creek.

As Dad drove, he gave us a history lecture about how Michigan got the Upper Peninsula as a booby prize after losing another piece of land to Ohio. While Dad went on and on, Jane was making "friendship rings" out of beads and thread and shoveling Oreo cookies into her mouth. She gave the rings to her Blue Bird friends, to her teachers, and to all her relatives. I already had at least two friendship rings on each finger and a bunch of her "friendship pins" on my shirts, sweaters, and shoelaces.

Meanwhile, I was drawing a cartoon of Mom and Dad in my sketchbook. In my drawing, Mom was staring out the car window with a spacy look in her blue-gray eyes and her notebook on her lap. Next to her head I drew a thought bulb that said I THINK I'LL WRITE AN ODE TO A SPEED-LIMIT SIGN. Sitting next to Mom I drew Dad with his long, curly, gray-black hair flopping about in the wind and the little smile he gets on his face when he's concentrating. The words spilling out of Dad's mouth were THIS IS GOING TO BE AN EDUCATIONAL VACATION, KIDS!

4

"Did you hear what I said?" Dad suddenly asked, when he finished his history lesson.

"Sure, Dad, it was interesting," I answered.

"How about you, Mademoiselle?" he asked Jane. "Do you know where we're going?"

"Uh—Upper Missouri? No, Upper Minnesota!" said Jane, smiling at me so that I would know she was teasing Dad for my benefit.

Thanks to my eight-year-old sister's sense of humor, we had to listen to an additional lesson. After that, I got Dad to turn on the radio. We listened for a while (Dad called the DJs "ignoramuses of the first order") and then, about the time the radio faded out, we stopped at an A&W in Tomahawk, Wisconsin, for root beer and hamburgers. After lunch, Mom got behind the wheel, Jane fell asleep on my shoulder, and I continued to draw until late in the afternoon when Dad said, "Look, kids!"

I looked up in time to see two deer staring at our car from the edge of the forest. Jane was still asleep, so I twisted her head in the direction of the deer and said, "Look, Morrie!" She thought I was teasing her (for once she was wrong), so she punched me in the stomach, groaned, and went back to sleep.

Soon after we saw the deer we stopped for dinner at a place along the highway, and soon after that we entered Upper Michigan. It turned out that Dad was right—there *was* nothing but forests, mountains, lakes, a few ski resorts, and scattered small towns up there.

Mom drove along the highway, which they call Highway

5

2, for quite a few miles before turning onto a dirt road called Copper Creek Road. A quarter mile or so down Copper Creek Road we came to a place where a bunch of old, white buildings stood. In front of the main building was a COPPER CREEK RESORT sign in glass letters. Except for the red *O* in RESORT, all the letters were burned out.

Mom turned onto the gravel driveway and brought the wagon to a crunching stop next to an old blue Cadillac convertible. There were four loud slams of doors as we got out of the car. "Well, peoples, old Calamity made it," Dad said, patting the car's hood.

Standing there gazing at the low purple mountains in one direction and the forest in the three other directions, I heard a strange sound. Only when a huge bird soaring over the mountains made a loud "*CAWWW!*" did I realize what it was. In the city there are continual voices and cars honking and trains whistling by and machines at work. Even in the middle of the night you can hear a kind of perpetual hum. But in front of Uncle Myron's resort it was *very, very* quiet.

Crap, a whole month of quiet and beauty, I thought. I felt really depressed as I went through my list of all I was going to be missing: fast-pitch games at Addison Park with my friend George Parkinson, blowing my allowance on video games at the Roscoe Street Seven-Eleven, TV (my parents had said our cottage had no TV), the Good Humor truck every night, the Chicago Cubs, taking the el downtown, and lots of other stuff.

A door with the word OFFICE on it opened, and a little

beagle dog ran out wagging its tail and crying as if we were its long-lost cousins. Jane and Mom and I were petting the dog when the office door again opened, and out walked a man.

It was twilight, so I couldn't tell much about him at first except to notice that he approached us eagerly. Once he was closer I saw that he was around sixty-five years old, about six foot one, and strong looking. He wore faded blue jeans and a checked flannel shirt open wide enough at the top so that his thick gray chest hairs were visible. His curly silver hair was long for a pretty old guy, and there was a grayish stubble on his cheeks that would have made him look tough if he hadn't been smiling.

After an awkward moment, Mom clasped his hands, looked up at his blue eyes, and said, "Uncle Myron!" As he said, "Leah!" and bent his head to kiss her, I noticed that Uncle Myron had a scar shaped like an upside-down **V** on his right cheek.

Mom introduced him to Dad, who said, "Great to see you again after all these years, Myron." Dad then pointed his finger toward the low range of mountains and added, "Even more magnificent than you said in your letter."

"Give Ma Nature the credit," Uncle Myron said. "But I will take credit for picking this place to live."

When Dad and Uncle Myron finished shaking hands, Uncle Myron came over to Jane and me. "Jane Monahan, I'm very glad to meet you. I'm your great-uncle Myron." As if it were the most natural thing in the world, he picked Jane up (a risky thing to do, because most kids hate being picked

7

up by people they've just met), gave her a quick kiss on the cheek, and put her back down before she could think.

"What's her name?" Jane asked, as she went back to petting Uncle Myron's little beagle dog.

"Randa," our uncle answered. Then he smiled at me with his whole face, put out his hand, and said: "Glad to have you here, Shelley. Last time I saw you, you were dipping a plastic *Tyrannosaurus rex* into the chopped liver at a Passover seder."

Before I continue, let me explain my background. Mom's Jewish. Dad's Irish-Catholic. About my name—Shelley Virgil Monahan. Shelley isn't for Sheldon. It's *Shelley*. Mom named me for her favorite poet—Percy Shelley. Sometimes at school, substitute teachers call me Sheldon and I have to explain that it really is Shelley. It's not that I'm crazy about the name. It's just that it's mine, and I like people to get it straight.

Virgil—my middle name—was Dad's idea. His favorite author is the Roman poet Virgil who wrote the *Aeneid*. I'm not thrilled about Virgil, either. Mom and Dad say that my name has dignity and that one day I'll appreciate it. You'll notice, however, that they named kid number two "Jane Miriam."

Mom kept nervously fingering the pencil in her frizzy hair as the five of us stood looking at each other. She couldn't write a poem standing there, though, so instead she started talking. When Mom's nervous she can instantly become a compulsive talker.

"Shelley, do you remember visiting Uncle Myron in that

big apartment near the lake?" she asked. Studying him closely, I thought I remembered a man with slicked-down hair and a fancy suit, but it was hard to believe that the guy in the checked shirt and faded jeans was the same person. "Do you know how Uncle Myron's related to you kids?" Mom then asked.

"He's your father's brother?" I answered hopefully.

"No, he's my mother's brother. You know Grandma Anna. Well, Uncle Myron's her baby bro—"

"Come on, I'll show you around the place," Uncle Myron said, taking Mom by the arm. As we walked toward the office and Randa ran off barking into the woods, I heard Uncle Myron quietly tell Mom: "Don't you remember how boring old relatives were when you were a kid, Leah?"

The brightly lit office contained a couple of old torn chairs, a front desk with a tall cash register on it, a cigarette machine that had no cigarettes, and a wall calendar that said JANUARY, 1980 (it was July, 1984).

"I live back here," Uncle Myron said, leading us behind the front desk and then into a room. The moment I saw his room I liked him. There were clothes, newspapers, books, a couple Nachos and Chee-tos bags, and pop cans on the floor. There were paintings of forest scenes on the walls, and near his bed was an easel with a half-done portrait of a raccoon on it.

Pointing to the painting on the easel, Jane said, "I do paint-by-numbers, too."

I gave Jane a kick in the leg and whispered, "Moron!" (my nickname for her). "Uncle Myron did those himself."

"I didn't know they weren't paint-by-numbers, Big Butt!" Jane said, making a fist and turning red in the face.

Uncle Myron placed his powerful arm around Jane and pulled her to him before she could slug me. "I'm sure they're not as good as your paint-by-numbers, Jane," he said, with a smile. "I just do it for fun."

Just then something caught my eye. At the end of Uncle Myron's unmade bed lay a small raccoon. Jane must have noticed it at the same time because she asked, "You have a pet *raccoon*?"

Uncle Myron nodded. "I found Nathan with an injured paw when he was a baby, and nursed him back to health. I took him down to the stream to let him go, but he just came back. Ten years ago I was selling coats made out of these guys, and now look at me."

"Uncle Myron used to be in the fur business," Dad explained.

For a couple minutes I looked at the little raccoon, which had the funniest way of staring right back at me. Finally Jane yawned, and Uncle Myron said, "I'll take you folks to your cottage."

He took a flashlight out of his desk drawer and a key off the rack, then led us back outside. Except for one time when we went to Mammoth Cave and the guy turned off the lights, I'd never been in a place so dark.

"I've never seen the stars like this before," said Mom, her voice sounding like she was about to cry.

I looked up, and there were zillions of stars sprinkled across the sky like different-colored lightning bugs. They looked so close I actually flinched. "I bet it'd look even better without that cloud down the middle," I said.

"That's not a cloud—it's the Milky Way," Uncle Myron explained. "One night we'll look at it through my telescope and you'll see that it's made of billions of stars."

"Moron!" Jane muttered, giving me a poke in the ribs. I *did* feel like a moron, too. Of course I'd heard of the Milky Way, but I'd never seen it in Chicago.

By the light of Uncle Myron's flashlight, I saw that cottages one through nine were small and unoccupied. Then we came to a white cottage with a red TEN over the door. As Uncle Myron unlocked the door, I observed that this one was the size of a regular house.

When the door swung open, Randa came running out of the woods and was the first one inside the cottage. "I couldn't get rid of the musty smell," Uncle Myron apologized, once we were inside. "There haven't been more than a couple guests in here for years."

While Dad brought the wagon up and Mom and Uncle Myron sat on the couch talking, Jane and I explored Cottage Ten with Randa. We loved the place, which had a kitchen, a living room, a bathroom, and three little bedrooms. When Dad returned with the two suitcases, Uncle Myron said "Good-night" and left with his dog.

Mom looked the place over and then announced: "Unless I hear a major objection, Dad and I will take the big bedroom, Jane gets the one with the clown-face lamp, and Shelley has the one with the bird drawings on the walls."

"Off to bed, you two weary-looking travelers," said Dad,

tossing us our pajamas from out of a suitcase. "Aren't you tired, Leah?" he then asked, handing Mom her nightgown. When he kissed her neck (Dad's so much shorter than Mom that her neck is where his mouth naturally reaches), Jane and I grinned at each other.

I hate to admit it, but I was really scared there that first night. When I went into the bathroom to get into my pajamas, I kept looking at the black square of darkness through the bathroom window. After we all kissed good-night and I was left alone in bed in my room, it got even worse. I'd been staring at the crack of night that showed between my curtains for about ten minutes when I heard Jane call: "I'm thirsty."

Dad grumbled and then cheerfully said, "I'm coming." I could hear the groan of the plumbing as Dad filled a glass with water. Between drinks Jane asked: "Do bears live around here, Daddy?"

"Probably, but they never *ever* come inside."

"Can you leave the door open so more light comes in?"

"Sure, sweetheart." The door creaked as he left her room and returned to Mom.

Lying there in bed, I explained to myself that it was dumb to be scared of robbers, bears, the dark, or anything else, but of course it didn't do any good. After lying there a while I sat up, poked my head under the curtains, and looked outside. The dark outline of the mountains was visible in the distance, and above it were countless stars. While I was looking outside I heard a snap of twigs in the forest, and then a loud bark close by. I closed the curtains and lay back down, even more scared.

I was lying there feeling that way when suddenly my door opened and there, standing over me, was a glowing head. I leaped up right on top of the bed and nearly banged my head on the ceiling, but then I saw that it was Jane with the glow of the bathroom light behind her. With a cry in her voice she whispered, "I'm scared here, Shelley. Could you sleep in the other bed in my room?"

"Sure," I said, barely able to talk.

I brought my pillow into her room and lay down on the extra bed. After I'd been there for a few minutes, Jane said, "You're really brave, Shelley."

"There's nothing to be scared of, Morrie," I explained, feeling better now that I had company. (When I'm feeling brotherly toward Jane, I call her Morrie—short for Moron.)

"I wish I was brave like you," she said. "Like after we saw that movie about the ghosts."

"You'll be brave, too, when you're my age," I said, remembering how I'd slept on the floor of her room for three nights without our folks knowing after that particular movie. "'Night, Morrie."

"'Night, Shelley," she said, and was soon snoring.

2

The Strange Blue Lights

Early the next morning, I was awakened by Jane jumping onto my bed and saying, "Shelley, I'll play checkers with you. I got them from the car." Jane knows I love checkers, and she wanted to thank me for sleeping with her by playing a few games—at seven A.M. according to the digital watch Grandma Anna had given me for my thirteenth birthday a couple months earlier.

After a few games Mom and Dad awoke, and we all got dressed and brought our stuff in from the car. My idea of fun *wasn't* being in the middle of nowhere for a month with my parents and my eight-year-old sister, so as I put my underwear in the drawers, I felt pretty "glum," to use one of Mom's words.

By about eight-thirty we were done unpacking and hungry. We figured Uncle Myron was still sleeping, so we piled into the wagon and headed for the nearest occupied town—Odell—about twelve miles away. See, the "town" where Uncle Myron's resort was located—Copper Creek—was really just an abandoned mining town. Uncle Myron and a couple dozen loggers, farmers, and retired miners lived scattered about, but the stores and businesses in the downtown part of Copper Creek had been boarded up for years.

The road to Odell took us through thick forest, up and down hills, and alongside mountains. We passed a couple farms chopped out of the forest, and Jane and I spotted some horses grazing in the fields. We passed a sign that said ODELL POP. 8427, and there—the morning sunlight glinting off the windows like a thousand diamonds—was a pretty little town nestled in the hills.

We drove up a hill and onto Iron Street, which was the town's main street. There we found a restaurant with a rusty ODELL DINER sign creaking in the breeze. The four of us sat down in a booth that had torn red upholstery and ordered juice, hash browns, and bacon and eggs.

Two people worked the place—a woman of about fifty and a girl around my age. The woman was friendly and asked where we were from. The girl had bright red hair, braces, freckles, and a pout. I knew she noticed me because she managed a polite smile for Dad, Mom, and Jane, but when her eyes met mine she blinked and then looked away. Girls usually don't notice me like that, so I was thrilled.

Embroidered on the girl's blue blouse was the name TRISH VINCENT. When Trish Vincent poured Dad a second cup of coffee, I said, "Nice breakfast," but she just gave me that pouty look and said, "Thanks." When Dad said, "Good coffee," she smiled and said, "Glad you liked it, sir."

After breakfast we explored Odell. Its hilly streets contained a hardware store, a grocery, a library, a barbershop, a

15

bank, a bicycle-sports shop, a dime store, an American Legion hall, and a couple churches. I couldn't find any game arcades, but there was a movie theater.

We went to the Big Dollar, where we bought a hundred dollars worth of groceries in twenty minutes. They were nice about it when I walked into the pyramid of Hawaiian Punch cans and knocked them down like bowling pins. I'd been thinking about Trish Vincent and hadn't been watching where I was going.

After the kid loaded the groceries into the tail of the wagon, we returned to the resort. Uncle Myron, wearing just a pair of brown shorts, was standing at his easel painting his raccoon's portrait while the animal sat on the ground next to him munching a bowlful of sliced carrots and M&M's.

"I meant to tell you last night that I had breakfast for you in the icebox," said Uncle Myron. In the morning sunlight, his eyes were as light blue as the cloudless summer sky and the silver hairs on his head, arms, and chest sparkled. His thick mat of chest hairs gave him a very masculine look, but there was something gentle about those almond-shaped blue eyes.

"Next time we go to breakfast, you're coming with us, Myron," Dad said. "It's fine of you to put us up like this."

"Don't be so grateful, James," Uncle Myron replied, "I'm happy to have your company."

* * *

16

I never figured I'd ever view my eight-year-old sister as my buddy, but that's exactly what she was on that vacation. We got the Wiffle ball and bat out of the wagon and had ball games on the gravel in front of our cottage. We also made games of tossing pebbles into a cup (basketball), knocking a tennis ball across Jane's room with rolled-up magazines (hockey), and flipping pennies into paper cups (tiddly-winks). One afternoon we taught Randa how to catch a Frisbee, and I even played jump rope and jacks with Jane. I got to see the kid's good qualities—persistence, for example. She'd chase ten home runs into the weeds and keep pitching until she got me out. Then late in the game while I was day-dreaming, she'd get a bunch of hits, and suddenly the score would be close.

About our third night there, Mom barbecued on the little grill we'd brought along and Dad made his famous Caesar salad. Uncle Myron joined us. I got to know him better that night. His last name was Silver and he'd been in the fur business in Chicago before retiring to Upper Michigan about ten years earlier. I liked the way his last name went with his silver hair. I liked his blue eyes, which were so gentle, and the faded tattoo on his left arm that said TILLIE next to a heart with an arrow through it. I especially enjoyed the way he used Yiddish expressions like "What a schmuck!"

After dinner, Uncle Myron and I went outside the cottage to put out the coals. As we poured water on them, Uncle Myron looked up at the star-filled sky and asked, "Maybe everyone would like to look through my telescope?"

17

We put on our jackets while Uncle Myron went to get his telescope. He came to get us, and with the quarter moon lighting our way, we walked to the spot near his office where he'd set it up.

My uncle aimed the telescope at the moon, which seemed closer and brighter than I'd ever seen it in Chicago. When it was my turn, I was amazed to see that the moon's craters and mountains looked close enough to touch.

"That's one of the loveliest things I've ever seen," Mom said, during her turn. She pulled out her paper and pen, and by the light of the moon jotted something down.

After we'd each seen the moon twice, Uncle Myron pointed the telescope at a bright white object that hung like a lantern between the moon and Indianface Mountain. "The planet Venus," Uncle Myron said.

"Named for the Roman goddess of love," Dad chimed in.

"Ahhhhh!" Mom said, as she looked at the white planet.

"Hurry up and let me see before it goes behind that cloud!" yelled Jane.

Just as I was about to view Venus, the broken clouds covered it like a net, blotting out some of its light. Then the planet disappeared completely, like a candle being blown out. "In a minute there'll be a break in the clouds and you'll get to see it," Uncle Myron told me.

We stood there shivering while waiting for the clouds to break. "Here it comes!" said Uncle Myron. He quickly focussed the telescope.

I was gazing at the crescent-shaped white planet when I

heard Dad say, "What in the world is *that*?"

I looked up from the telescope where Dad was pointing. There, just above the peak of Indianface Mountain, were several blue lights. They hovered over the mountain for maybe twenty seconds. Suddenly they zoomed high above the mountain, then just as suddenly dropped back down.

"Is that a UFO?" my sister asked.

"I've seen lights like that before a couple times," said Uncle Myron. "So has my friend Harv Holmquist. I think they're a reflection from somewhere bouncing off the clouds or off the mountain."

"To me it looks like it's a light rather than a reflection, Myron," said Mom.

"It's a UFO! It's a UFO!" Jane yelled.

"I don't know what it is, but I don't believe in flying saucers," said Uncle Myron. "Look—" The blue lights suddenly zoomed straight up, disappearing above the clouds.

"Wait until we get home and tell everyone we saw a flying saucer!" said Jane, who was the most excited of us.

I didn't believe in flying saucers for one main reason. Most of the people who claim to have spotted them seem like crackpots. They usually sell their stories to those weeklies you see at checkout counters—you know, the ones with headlines like WOMAN GIVES BIRTH TO CHIMPANZEE TRIPLETS and NEW PROOF THAT ELVIS PRESLEY IS ALIVE. There was another reason I didn't pay much attention to the blue lights. My mind was more on Trish Vincent than on stuff like that.

19

Not wanting to ruin Jane's excitement, I said, "Well, it really is a UFO because UFO means 'unidentified flying object,' and we don't know what it is."

The day we saw the blue lights was July 27, 1984. I know because I jotted down a couple sentences about it in my diary.

3

Trish Vincent

W e'd been on vacation for about a week when the folks were ready to go back to Odell. "You kids can stay here and play if you want," Dad said, before we left the cottage. I paused as if thinking about it and then said, "We might as well go along, Morrie."

Once in Odell, the first thing we did was get a family summer card for one dollar at the Odell Carnegie Library. Dad was excited about the library because it contained books from the 1800s. "They don't make encyclopedias like this anymore," he said, blowing the dust off a volume. "Look at those details."

After glancing through the C volume, I said, "It says Grover Cleveland is president, Dad."

While Dad was getting high from the dusty books in the reference room, Mom led us downstairs to the children's section. "Look, an ancient edition of *The Wizard of Oz*— and here's the Moffat books I loved when I was a kid. Why don't you kids stay here and read while I go to the laundry?"

21

I grabbed a couple Moffat books and shoved three Dr. Seusses into Jane's hands. "We've got our books. I'd like to walk around town a while."

"Fine," said Mom. "Tell Dad we'll all meet at the car at ten forty-five."

I was hoping Jane would go to the laundry with Mom, but as Mom went to get the shopping bags with the dirty clothes out of the wagon, Jane said, "I'm going with Shelley."

You can imagine how thrilled I was to have my little sister accompany me. Jane had to run to keep up as I walked the two blocks from the library to the diner. Once there, I slowed down and entered nonchalantly. As we sat down, Jane said, "That girl with the red hair looks like the one you've been drawing."

"Jane Miriam Monahan, *shut up!*" I said.

Just then Trish Vincent, wearing her cute blue blouse, white jeans, and red-and-blue striped apron, walked up to take our order. I smiled at her when she handed us our menus, but she didn't smile back. "I'd like a Coke."

"Me, too," said Jane.

I studied Trish Vincent as she pushed open the swinging counter door and then sprayed Coke into two glasses with the thing that looks like the end of a garden hose. Her eyes seemed more violet than blue and went really nicely with her red hair and freckles. She also had the tiniest bit of cute plumpness. (I'm about nine and a half pounds overweight, and I'm partial to people who aren't thin.)

Usually I'm too shy to talk much to girls, but when you're a stranger in town you feel like you can act out of character.

22

See, nobody there knew that I was shy. When she brought us the Cokes, I said, "My name's Shelley Monahan. What's yours?"

"Trish Vincent, just like it says," she said, pointing to the writing on her blouse.

"That's the name you've been writing on the drawings," Jane said.

Did you ever feel like you could strangle someone? As Trish walked away, I said, "My sister's confusing you with another Trish." I sat trying to think up a way to make her come back without being too obvious about it. "Could you please make this a cherry Coke?" I called out.

I feared she'd get annoyed, but she came back to get my glass, went behind the counter, and squirted some red into it. When she brought me my cherry Coke, Jane said, "Could you do that in mine, too, Trish?"

Trish gave her a big smile that showed a lot of her braces. "Sure, hon. What's your name?"

"Jane. Jane Monahan. Jane Miriam Monahan."

"She's my little sister."

Still looking at Jane, Trish asked: "Where do you live?"

"In Chicago," Jane answered. "We're on vacation."

"That's nice." Trish took Jane's Coke and filled it high with cherry. She brought it to Jane, gave her another lovely smile, and then went to pour coffee for an elderly man who was sitting at the counter reading a newspaper.

"She's nice," said Jane.

"Yeah," I said, studying Jane's short, curly, brownish

blonde hair and brown eyes to see if I could figure out how she'd gotten those big smiles from Trish.

I felt pretty glum as we waited in the wagon for our folks. In eighth grade there had been lots of guys who had walked with their arms around girls' waists. This was almost the first time I'd even tried to speak to a girl, and she had liked my little sister better than me.

When we got home, Jane and I had a Wiffle ball game before lunch. She belted one about twenty feet into the weeds, and I pretended it was lost so she could get a home run. While she was circling the bases, I picked up a sharp rock and quickly carved

S.V.M.

+

T.V.

on the back of a tree. While I was finishing the *V*, Jane came up to me and said, "The ball's right at your feet." She looked at the initials, thought a moment, and then said: "I'll make a friendship ring for you to give her."

"You'd better give it to her yourself because I don't think she'd take it from me."

After lunch I still felt glum, so I asked Jane if she wanted to take the hike down to the stream Uncle Myron had mentioned the night of the barbecue. We found him outside working on his portrait of Nathan. When we asked him about the hike, Uncle Myron smiled, placed his paintbrush on the easel, and told us to put on jackets and our worst shoes and meet him outside the office in a couple minutes.

When we came back outside, we found Uncle Myron wearing a red-and-black lumber jacket and tall hiking boots. Randa was sitting patiently by his side and Nathan was a little way down the ravine behind the office. We followed our uncle and his two pets down the ravine, which was so steep that we had to grab onto tree limbs and roots to keep from falling. Halfway down, Randa sniffed at some tracks, then picked up her head to howl at the treetops.

"Are those bear tracks?" Jane asked.

"Deer—a doe and two fawns, it looks like," Uncle Myron explained. On the way to the stream, he also told us the names of the wildflowers and the trees. He even knew the birds by their calls.

"How'd you learn all that?" I asked.

"Some I learned from my friend Harv Holmquist when we've gone hunting, and some I picked up from books."

"Why'd you name him Nathan?" asked Jane, pointing to the raccoon who was ahead of us, but behind Randa.

"When I was in the fur business, my partner's name was Nathan," our uncle answered.

We had a fine time down at the stream, which was called Copper Creek. There were little toads down there, and tiny fish you could barely see even when you looked right at them, and even a little waterfall where the frothy reddish water passed over some rocks.

Nathan perched himself on a rock in the stream and stared down at the water with his serious brown eyes. From

25

time to time he dipped his paw into the water, and when he caught a fish he'd pop it into his mouth to eat it. Randa, meanwhile, was happily splashing around the stream. When she came out and shook herself off, the spray made a pretty rainbow that lasted for a second.

On the way up, as Uncle Myron helped Jane make a wild-flower bouquet for Mom, my sister told our uncle that he reminded her of Grizzly Adams.

"Who's that?" he asked.

"A character in an old TV show," I explained.

"I've got a TV but I never watch it. I suppose I could get the stations from Odell and Duluth."

Jane and I stared at each other. "A TV?" we both repeated.

"You can use it—if it's okay with your parents."

We went uphill faster than we'd gone down. When we asked our parents about it, they went into their bedroom for a conference. The verdict was that we could watch only an hour or two a day and we had to watch the educational station half the time if it came in there. We were allowed to bring the TV into Cottage One, right next to the office—and that was how Jane and I got our own place, complete with TV.

Fortunately, we could barely get the educational station from Green Bay, Wisconsin, because there was no outside antenna. We did get two channels clearly—WTRZ in Duluth, Minnesota, and WKRL in Odell. We watched a lot more than two hours a day, but Mom and Dad didn't say anything because they could sleep late and work in peace. In the morning, while Jane made her friendship rings and I drew cartoons, we'd watch "Popeye," "I Love Lucy," "Bugs Bunny," "Tom and Jerry," "Lost in Space," and the old "Superman." In the afternoon we'd watch "Star Trek," "The Twilight Zone," "Happy Days," and "The Brady Bunch."

One morning Uncle Myron came in with some pop and popcorn and sat down to watch a little TV with us. "I forgot what *chozzerai* (Mom later told us that's a Yiddish word meaning "garbage") they show," Uncle Myron told us. A few minutes later there was a scratch at the door. It was Nathan. The raccoon had been pretty shy with us at first, but I guess he had a weakness for popcorn, because he climbed right onto the couch and dug into the popcorn bowl. After that, Uncle Myron would bring us popcorn and watch a little TV with us just about every day, and Nathan would come with him and help us eat the popcorn. Nathan was a pretty serious guy—we didn't roll around on the floor or stuff like that—but it was fun to have staring contests with him and be with him and Uncle Myron.

The second week of our stay, Uncle Myron invited us for a barbecue and we got to meet his friends Harv and Betty Holmquist. Harv, who owned a logging business, was an enormous guy who laughed a lot and wore giant-sized blue-jean overalls. He and Betty lived on a farm near Indianface Mountain about a mile and a half from Uncle Myron's place.

Harv had brought a bottle of blackberry wine he'd made. He poured it into Green Bay Packers mugs for all the adults except Uncle Myron, who said he couldn't drink it because of his ulcer. "You should'a seen Copper Creek in the days when the mine was going," Harv told Mom and Dad. "Why, in downtown Copper Creek they had a saloon called the Ore Haus and—"

"Harv, the children," said Betty, who was a small, blonde, sweet-looking woman.

"There's a downtown Copper Creek?" I asked.

"There used to be—before the mine closed," Harv answered, taking a bite into his fifth or sixth hamburger. "Let's take them there tomorrow, Mike."

"Okay," said Uncle Myron.

Late the next afternoon, Harv Holmquist stopped by in his green pickup and took us to see the abandoned copper mine. Then he drove us to "downtown" Copper Creek. It was a ghost town with a couple abandoned stores and buildings but no people. "Soon after your Uncle Mike bought the resort, the mine closed and everyone except the cuckoo ones moved away," Harv explained, with a loud laugh.

Harv then took us to the Holmquist farm near Indianface Mountain, where Betty raised bees for the honey she sold to the health shop in Odell. There were zillions of bees all over the place, but Betty taught us that if we didn't scare them by moving suddenly, they wouldn't sting.

Once a week Harv came over to play cards with Uncle Myron. On one of their card-playing nights, Mom and Dad went out to a movie, so Jane and I got to spend the evening in Uncle Myron's room watching the two men play gin rummy.

While they played, Jane and I and Nathan ate the popcorn Uncle Myron had made. Harv kept drinking blackberry wine and saying that Myron was thirty-one cents ahead because he was only drinking root beer. Uncle Myron said Harv was such a pitiful gin rummy player that he wouldn't be able to beat Jane or me. So they taught us the game, and we beat both of them. I made nearly fifty cents that night.

The truth was, I was having a lot better time than I'd expected, but what I really looked forward to was going back to Odell. I changed underwear twice a day to make laundry day come quicker. Finally, when we'd been there two weeks, Mom and Dad decided it was time to go to town again. Dad had seen in Uncle Myron's Odell *Daily Globe* that *Bambi* was playing at the Odell Theatre, and the folks said they'd treat us to a movie after we finished our chores.

Jane and I helped Mom shop and do laundry while Dad did his library work. When it was time for the movie, I said, "I'll be embarrassed being the oldest kid in the theater. I'd like to hang around town a while. I'll meet you when the movie's over."

Mom and Dad looked at each other. Then they both shrugged, and Mom said, "Sure." Jane quickly dug something out of her jeans pocket and handed it to me. "You can give it to Trish," she said. Of course, it was a friendship ring.

While they went to the theater, I strode over to the Odell Diner. It felt good being on my own with a couple bucks in my pocket and my family out of sight. As I sat down in my red, torn-leather booth, the older woman started to come over to take my order. Trish Vincent said something to her. My heart leaped as Trish came over herself.

"Cherry Coke?" Trish asked. She was wearing her cute red-and-blue apron, and her red hair was back in a ponytail. She had a pouty expression, as though she disliked being there.

"Lots of cherry, please," I said.

As she walked away, her ponytail flipped from side to side. When she brought me my cherry Coke, I said the only thing I could think of: "How old are you?"

"Thirteen. How about you?"

"Almost fourteen," I said, even though I'd just turned thirteen on April 15. "Were you born in Odell?"

"We're from Detroit," she said. "My Dad and I moved up here in January when he got laid off from the auto plant. He's working as a logger."

"Is that your mom?" I asked, pointing to the woman behind the counter.

"My aunt Theresa. My mom's dead, and we're living with my aunt. This is her place."

I glanced at Aunt Theresa, who was a heavyset woman with blonde hair that was so light it looked white.

"What's there to do in this town?" I asked Trish.

"Nothing much," she quickly answered.

"In Chicago we have lots to do," I said. "We have game arcades and movie theaters and kids all over the place."

"If it's so great, why'd you come here?"

"My folks made us. Oh, yeah," I added, pulling the

friendship ring out of my shirt pocket. "Remember my little sister? She made this for you."

Trish Vincent held the ring in her hand and then placed it on her finger. "It's beautiful," she said. "Tell Jane I love it."

My heart began to pound as I said, "It's almost five o'clock. What time do you get off work?"

"Five," she said, glancing at the old yellow wall clock.

"Could I walk you home?"

She thought a moment, then smiled and said: "Sure. I'll just be a minute."

Trish taking off her red-and-blue apron was the most exciting thing I'd ever seen. But as we walked outside I did something really stupid. I hardly know how to explain it. All I can say is I suddenly wanted to put my arm around her waist, and I just did it. The instant I put my arm there, she pushed it off, turned as red as her hair, and said, "What are you doing?"

"I—I—" I stammered, but she was already heading into an entranceway next door to the diner. "Wait a second, can't I still walk you home?"

"I *am* home. We live in an apartment right over the restaurant. I *was* going to ask you to come upstairs." She then went inside and climbed the stairs. I stood there watching from the sidewalk as she came to the window and pulled down the shades. I wanted to tell her I'm not the kind of guy who puts my arm around girls I hardly know and that I just did it because I suddenly wanted to a lot. Only I knew she'd never talk to me again.

31

I walked around town thinking about what had happened and finally found my way to the movie theater. I sat on the curb until the movie let out. "What happened to *you*, chum?" Dad asked, as they came out of the theater.

"Nothing," I said. But it took all my willpower to keep from breaking into tears.

4

The Flying Saucer Lands

I didn't go with the family when they went to town after that, because I couldn't bear to see the Odell Diner and know that *she* was in there hating me. When my family returned from town one day and Jane said, "That girl Trish thanked me for the friendship ring," I felt even worse.

One night in mid-August, Mom and Dad were working at the living-room table and Jane and I were on the floor playing Monopoly when Uncle Myron knocked on the door. "Harv and I just finished playing cards and we noticed the sky is clear," he said. "I thought you might like to come outside and look through my telescope."

We dressed in sweaters and jackets. Then, with his flashlight lighting our way, Uncle Myron led us to the spot near the office where he'd set up his telescope. He had also set up six lawn chairs and a table with plastic glasses and thermoses on it.

"Isn't that sky something?" asked Harv Holmquist, who was sitting on a lawn chair with a bottle in his hand.

Uncle Myron showed us Venus, as he had the last time.

We all went "Ahhh!" and "Beautiful!" but Harv said, "That ain't nothin'. Show them the one with the rings, Mike."

I actually gasped when I saw Saturn. It had a ring so perfect it didn't seem real. "Beautiful, just beautiful," Mom said. "Yah, that one's good," agreed Harv Holmquist.

While Harv drank blackberry wine and the rest of us drank hot chocolate, Uncle Myron showed us star clusters and nebulae. He let us sweep the telescope across the Milky Way while we looked through it. Doing that, I could see millions of sparkling blue, red, yellow, and white stars.

As Uncle Myron showed us the Ring nebula, Jane yawned and Harv said, "Yah, Jane, I'm sleepy, too. Guess I better think about heading home." Mom and Dad said they were ready to go to bed, but I said, "I'm not tired."

"If it's okay with you, I'll show Shelley a couple more things and then bring him inside," Uncle Myron said, after Harv had driven away in his pickup.

After Mom, Dad, and Jane went inside, Uncle Myron showed me the Andromeda galaxy and explained that the universe is made of billions of galaxies, each made of billions of stars. When he'd finished telling me about black holes, constellations, and some other things, I asked: "Did you learn all that when you were a kid?"

"I read it in books after I moved up here."

"When was that?"

"Almost ten years ago. I guess you're wondering why I live—look! Shooting star near Deneb."

We watched the shooting star streak across the sky. Uncle Myron explained that shooting stars are really just pebbles burning up in Earth's atmosphere and that August is a big month for seeing them. Then I said, "I *was* wondering why you live up here." I got up the courage to add, "And I was wondering how you got that scar on your cheek."

"World War II, which is a good place to begin," Uncle Myron said. "After the war ended, I went into the retail fur business in Chicago. The store made me rich—in fact, eventually I had three stores. I was a millionaire by the time I was forty—look there!"

"A millionaire," I repeated, as the shooting star streaked through the constellation that he'd just taught me was named Draco.

"Sure, but I worked sixty, seventy hours a week. I was always running from one store to the other and pacing floors at night, figuring how to do better. I told myself I was working hard so that Tillie and I could have the fine things of life someday—you know, fancy cars, a nice apartment, vacations—and that I'd spend more time with her once I could afford to. We got all that stuff, but I didn't slow down. It was nice to make more and more money, and besides, after a while it was the only thing I knew.

"Then in 1974, my wife got cancer and died. Do you remember Aunt Tillie?" As I shook my head, I noticed in the starlight that his eyes were glistening with moisture. "No, you wouldn't. You were just about three years old. When she died, I realized I'd been so busy becoming rich I'd hardly spent time with her. Now it was too late.

"With Tillie gone and with us having no children, I had no reason to keep working so hard, yet I kept going to the store every morning at six and working harder than ever. I didn't know how to do anything else. About six months after my wife passed away, I had a heart attack and nearly died myself. In fact, when I was in the coma or whatever, I remember thinking it'd be just as well if I did—"

He was silent for a while, so I asked, "If you did what?"

"I shouldn't go on like this. I made up my mind before you people came I wasn't going to burden you with ancient stories."

"But I still don't know why you came up here."

He sighed and then continued. "When I recovered from my heart attack, I decided to get away from everything. I saw an ad for this old resort in the *Tribune* and bought it. At the time, the mine was still going and some of the miners lived right here at my resort. But about eight years ago, the mine closed and most of the miners moved away to Odell or elsewhere. All I get now are hunters, lost tourists, and a few skiers in winter when the ski lodges on Indianface fill up."

"Why'd you stay?"

For a long time Uncle Myron was silent. Then he said, "I was a bitter man when I first came here. I didn't want to do anything or see anyone. I guess I was pretty depressed. Gradually I took up painting and astronomy, and then I even made friends—the Holmquists. It sounds corny, but at the age of sixty I discovered myself. I was a guy who could enjoy nature and painting and looking at the stars. It didn't matter that the resort business was lousy because I didn't

36

need the money. So I stayed. That's my story, Shelley."

As we sat there beneath the stars, I felt completely tuned in to Uncle Myron. I was thinking about all he'd told me when I saw several blue, glowing lights coming over the top of Indianface Mountain and moving slowly in our direction. I noticed them before Uncle Myron did, and yelled, "Look!" They were the same blue lights we'd seen before, only now they were coming toward us. In a few seconds, we could see that there were six of them in the shape of a circle.

Uncle Myron and I both stood up from the lawn chairs as the six blue lights approached. For an instant I thought they might be part of an advertising plane, but then they came closer and I saw it just as clear as could be. It was a round ship, a flying saucer, with blue lights on its underside. I could even see the windows along the rim when it went over our heads.

"It must be less than a hundred feet up!" Uncle Myron said as it went over. His face and everything around us was bathed in the blue lights of the saucer. Then the ship glided away over the forest, and Uncle Myron said, "Come on!"

As I followed Uncle Myron into the forest, I felt as if I was in one of those dreams where your legs can't move. I followed his flashlight beam and found myself standing next to him on a small bluff. From there, we watched the blue-lit saucer slowly descend into the forest in front of the next ridge of mountains.

"It must have landed three or four miles off," Uncle Myron said, "because those mountains are ten miles away, and it's well in front of them."

The glow of the blue lights was visible on the forest floor for a few seconds. Then suddenly the lights went out. I hadn't been scared when the saucer had passed overhead, but now I was shaking. We looked into the darkness for a while longer, and then I followed Uncle Myron back to the office.

"What do you think it was?" he asked me. But before I could answer, he said, "It must be something the government is testing—a new kind of weapon or space ship or something like that. No, that doesn't make sense. Shelley, what do you think it was?"

"A flying saucer—just like I've seen in movies and newspaper photographs. What if they saw us when they passed over and decide to come after us?"

"If they were after us, they wouldn't have landed so far away," my uncle answered.

"What should we do, Uncle Myron?" I asked.

"We should report it, but we'll never get anyone to go out there and investigate tonight. I'll come over to your place tomorrow morning and we'll tell your Mom and Dad about it, and then we'll go to the police."

Uncle Myron walked back to Cottage Ten with me. I got in bed fully dressed and lay there trembling most of the night. Maybe a hundred times I opened the curtains to see if anything was out there. Once when I dozed off for a couple minutes, I was awakened by a sound outside. I went to the window and looked outside, and there were two brown eyes staring right at me.

I was so scared, I tumbled right off the bed. I was about to crawl out of the room when I realized that I knew those eyes. I opened the curtains again, and sure enough, Nathan, the raccoon, was walking around outside the cottage. Not long after that it began to get light.

The next morning at breakfast, Mom saw me staring at the window and asked, "Are you feeling all right, Shelley?"

I didn't want to scare Jane by mentioning the flying saucer, so I said, "I think I stayed up too late reading." But after breakfast, when Jane asked me to go down to the river to search for pretty stones, I said, "Do you mind going into your room for a couple minutes, Mor? I want to tell Mom and Dad something private." Then, while Mom and Dad did the dishes, I said: "I—I saw something strange last night with Uncle Myron."

"What?" Mom asked, as she dried a dish.

"Well—there were these blue lights in the sky the same as the other night, only this time they came a lot closer and—"

Just then there was a knock on the door. "Come in," Dad said. My heart pounded as the door opened, but it was only Uncle Myron. "Have you told them?" he asked.

"I was telling them now." I then told my parents the whole story.

"It happened just as Shelley told it," said Uncle Myron. "We both saw it just as clearly as you can see that pine tree through that window."

"See, I *told* you we saw a flying saucer the other day," said

Jane, who had come out of her room to use the bathroom and had stopped in the hallway to listen.

"Maybe it was an airplane or helicopter," Dad said. "I think there's an Air Force base in Marquette. Maybe—"

Uncle Myron shook his head. "It was some kind of a space ship, Jim. I don't know if anybody will believe us, but a thing like this has to be reported."

"Absolutely!" agreed Mom.

The five of us got into our wagon and drove to the Odell Police Department, which was housed along with the fire department in a brick garage next to the library. It was Sunday and the building was locked, but a sign on the door listed an emergency number, which Uncle Myron called from the phone outside the library.

About five minutes later, a big, gray-haired man with his stomach hanging over his belt came slowly up the street. With only a nod, he unlocked the door and led us past a fire truck to a cubicle with the words ODELL POLICE DEPT. on it. He sat down at a desk with a plaque that said EARL G. McMASTER, CHIEF OF POLICE. "How can I help you?" he asked, with a weak smile.

As soon as Uncle Myron began the story, the smile left the chief's face. When Uncle Myron neared the end of the story, the chief began to rifle through his desk. He pulled stacks of official forms out of several drawers and flipped through them while shaking his head. Finally he took an old loose-leaf notebook from the bottom drawer and ripped a sheet out of it.

After writing down our names, our addresses, and some

information about our story, the chief asked us a few questions: what time did we see it, did anyone else see it with us, and stuff like that. Then the chief said, "Well, thanks a lot for coming in."

"That's all?" Mom asked. "You're not going to do anything else about it?"

"What more can I do?" asked the chief, looking annoyed at her.

"Go out and look for the place where it landed!" Mom answered, even more annoyed.

"Ever since we had the budget cut, except for a guy who works part-time, *I'm* the Odell Police Department," said the chief. "If I leave to go look for a flying saucer and something happens here in town while I'm—Look, folks, I've written a report, but that's all I can do."

"You don't believe us!" said Uncle Myron angrily. "If you believed us you'd find time to go out there and look for it!"

"It's not that I don't believe you. It's just that late at night your eyes can play tricks on you, and you can mistake an airplane—"

We all stalked out of there. "Maybe we should write a letter to the Air Force," said Mom, as we drove back to the resort. "Other than that, about all we can do is keep our eyes open."

When we got back to the resort, Uncle Myron and I talked it over and decided to call the Odell *Daily Globe*. Without giving the receptionist his name, Uncle Myron asked if anyone else had reported a flying saucer. No one

41

else had. He then said he had a very important story to report and asked to speak to an editor. My hopes grew as Uncle Myron related the entire story. But after he finished, Uncle Myron listened for a minute and then scowled. "You don't believe me, do you? I'm telling you one of the biggest news stories you've ever had, and you just think I'm making it up. All right, all right, good-*bye!*" he said angrily, and hung up the phone in disgust.

"He said they don't run flying saucer stories," Uncle Myron told me. "He listened to the whole thing just to humor me."

That afternoon, Uncle Myron and I got in his old Cadillac convertible and headed in the direction of where we'd seen the UFO land. We explored some dirt roads and looked through the forest as we drove along, but we didn't find a trace of the saucer. When we got back, Uncle Myron and I gave Mom a detailed description of what we'd seen, and she wrote it down and sent it to the Air Force.

We kept our eyes open the rest of our stay, but we didn't see anything strange. A couple days before the end of our vacation, one unusual event did occur. One morning when Jane and I went to Cottage One to watch TV, we found the window open. The TV—but nothing else—was gone.

"That's the darnedest thing," said Uncle Myron. "We haven't had a robbery in all the years I've owned this place—not counting a few towels."

The day we reported the missing TV was the day we made our last visit to Odell. I walked right past the Odell Diner and saw Trish Vincent in there behind the counter.

She looked right at me, but then quickly turned away.

I only tried to put my arm around her, I thought.

The next day we said good-bye to Uncle Myron. He invited us to come back the next year, and then we climbed into Calamity and headed for home.

I felt sad leaving Upper Michigan, and sadder and sadder the closer we got to Chicago. I missed Uncle Myron already, I missed not being near Trish Vincent, and I wondered if anything was going to come of the UFO we'd seen land in the forest.

5

No One Believes Me

Let's say someone had come up to me before that summer began and said: "I saw a flying saucer go right over my head." You know what I would have said? I would have said, "*Sure* you did." Even if the person passed a lie detector test and repeated the story under hypnosis, I still would have said, "*Sure.*" See, I hadn't believed in flying saucers. After my UFO experience, all that was changed. The problem was that there were lots of other people who would say "*Sure!*" if I told them about it.

The first thing I had to do was find a way to tell people about it. From the night I'd seen the UFO go overhead, I'd wanted to tell everyone, but it wasn't so easy to do. I mean, you don't go up to your aunt Mildred or your Sunday School teacher and say: "By the way, a UFO went over my head while I was out in the country."

The first person I told about the UFO was my best friend, George Parkinson. It was a very sad time—the day before we were to begin freshman year of high school. We were playing fast-pitch against the field house wall at Addison

44

Park, which is close to Wrigley Field. Anyway, in the distance, Parkinson and I heard the roar of the crowd and then a louder roar. "Sandberg or Cey must have put one in orbit," Park said, reaching his hand out for the bat.

At that moment I decided to tell him. "George, this really weird thing happened in the country," I said. Park and I had been buddies a long time. We'd been in Little League together, gone to the Unitarian Sunday School together, made a movie together for eighth-grade Fine Arts (George acted in it and I shot it), cheated on tests together at school, and spent a lot of time at each other's houses. But George can be real sarcastic, so I was worried about how he'd react.

We walked over to the playground and found a shady spot on the edge of the sandbox. "Well, it all started one night when we saw these blue lights in the sky," I began, and then told him the rest of the story. I even drew a picture of the UFO with my finger in the sand. Park sat open-mouthed and then said, "I'd give half the gray matter in my brain to have seen that with you, Shelley. Were you scared?"

"Out of my mind," I answered, thinking what a true friend Parkinson was. Just because *I* had told it to him, he didn't have the slightest doubt about the story.

In a way, it's not right to call this chapter "No One Believes Me." Park believed me and so did my sister and of course Uncle Myron. My parents believed me—at least it seemed like Mom did. It was more or less the people I didn't know—the important people—who didn't believe me.

The first problem I had about it occurred in English class. You know those How-I-spent-my-summer-vacation essays? My English teacher, Mr. Munk, said that he thought those essays were boring. We got our hopes up, but then he told us to write a four-hundred-word essay on "My Most Interesting Experience This Summer" and smiled as if there were something original about the assignment.

Aside from when I'd told Park, that was the first time I described my UFO experience after returning to Chicago. I thought I wrote a terrific paper, but I got a C.

"Mr. Monahan, this was supposed to be a *nonfiction* paper describing a TRUE event," Mr. Munk wrote, and underlined "TRUE" three times. I knew it was dumb to talk to him about the UFO, but I didn't want to start freshman English with a C. After class I got up the courage to join the other students at Mr. Munk's desk who were asking about their grades.

"I don't think I got a fair grade, sir," I told him, when it was my turn. "I wrote a true paper, just like you said, and I didn't make very many mistakes."

Looking very surprised, Mr. Munk said, "Oh—oh my, a *true* paper," and then added, "May I see it again?" He rolled the sleeves of his pink shirt up past his little elbows and reread it as several of my classmates looked on. After making a couple corrections, he wrote a B– on the paper and then handed it back to me. As I walked out the door, Mr. Munk smiled the way you might smile at a crazy person.

The worst part of it was that my whole English class got wind of the fact that I'd seen "a space ship go right over my head," as several kids pointed out. It's hard to describe the razzing I got after that. A few guys near my locker began to call me "spaceman," and when I threw the ball out of bounds in gym, someone said, "He's throwing it to that little green man over there—don't you see him?" In Social Studies, before Mr. Greenebaum came in, kids threw paper rockets at me and said, "Look out, there's a flying saucer going right over your head!" Understand, George Parkinson and my other friends from eighth grade didn't join in, but enough kids did to make my life rough.

A couple weeks after school began, we received this letter from the Air Force:

September 25, 1984

Mrs. Leah Monahan
1123 Sinclair St.
Chicago, Illinois 60613

Dear Mrs. Monahan:

This is in response to your August 20, 1984, letter regarding Unidentified Flying Objects (UFOs).

Although we are grateful that you took the time to write, the Air Force is no longer investigating reports of UFOs. Between 1948 and 1969—in a program known for most of the time as "Project Blue Book"—the Air Force investigated 12,618 reported sightings. Only 701 of those could not be explained. The Air Force terminated Blue Book in December of 1969 because no evidence had been found that the sightings involved spacecraft from other worlds or were in any way a threat to national security.

All Blue Book documents are in the National
Archives where they are available to the public.
Thanks again for your thoughtful letter regarding
this complex topic.

Sincerely,

John V. Roche, Jr.

John V. Roche, Jr., Major, USAF
Assistant Chief
Civil Affairs Branch
Community Relations Division
Office of Public Affairs

Attachments

One of the attachments explained how most of the 12,618 sightings studied between 1948 and 1969 turned out to be "aircraft, weather balloons, satellites, atmospheric illusions, and hoaxes." Another listed names and addresses of private UFO study organizations.

It's pretty frustrating when you saw a UFO land and your mother sent a letter about it, and your own country's Air Force doesn't seem to care. After that it occurred to me that astronomers might be the ones to tell about the UFO, so I went to the library, looked up a couple, and wrote to them in care of their book publishers. I also wrote letters about it to several newspapers and magazines.

Most of my letters weren't even answered, but one day when I came home from school I was excited to find a letter from an astronomer I'd seen on TV. I still have his letter in my drawer, right next to the one from the Air Force:

November 6, 1984

Mr. Shelley Monahan
1123 Sinclair St.
Chicago, Illinois 60613

Dear Shelley:

I'm so glad to have gotten a letter from a budding astronomer. It sounds like your uncle Myron has done a fine job teaching you about the constellations and night sky. In fact, your careful observations of the conditions during the night of your "UFO" sighting have helped me to make an educated guess about what you saw.

You mentioned that you made your observation on the night of August 11. You also mentioned that you saw several meteors (commonly called "shooting stars") on that night. It happens that August 11 is the maximum night for the greatest meteor shower of the year. They are called the *Perseids* because they radiate from the constellation Perseus.

As you probably know, meteors are chunks of rock and metal which burn up when they strike Earth's atmosphere. I think the "six blue lights" you saw were a very bright meteor called a "fireball." Fireballs sometimes break apart as they collide with Earth's atmosphere, and this may be why you saw six separate lights. The blue color could have been caused by atmospheric distortion.

I don't have such an easy answer for the fact that you saw what looked like "a space ship go directly over our heads." But possibly, as the fireball went over, in your excitement you and your uncle thought you were seeing a spaceship. The glow in the forest could have been a

49

still-glowing piece of meteorite (which is what we call meteors that hit the ground), but, most likely, you saw the glow of a far-off house or campfire and connected it mentally with what you saw go overhead.

I'm sorry if this sounds like I'm trying to "explain away" what you saw, but in all the years since UFOs first became popular there has not been one iota of concrete proof that they are from outer space, and you will find very few, if any, astronomers who believe in them.

If you're ever in the area please look me up, and feel free to write any time.

With kindest regards,

Frank Jaspar

A. Francis "Frank" Jaspar

I felt so frustrated after getting that letter that I asked Mom and Dad if I could call Uncle Myron. For the first few minutes of our conversation, he asked me about school and I asked how his pets were and stuff like that. Then I told him about the letters from the Air Force and the astronomer.

"I did manage to interest someone in the story," Uncle Myron told me. "Shortly after you folks left I got to thinking that what we'd seen was just too important for people not to know about, so I called the TV station in Odell. I talked to an announcer you've probably seen, Ollie Rasmusson. He came over with a cameraman and interviewed me. Rasmusson told me that he'd gotten another call from someone who had seen it, but hadn't even written down the person's name since it sounded like a crackpot story. Since I was the second call, he started to take it seriously. I took him out to the place where we thought the flying saucer landed and everything. I waited a couple nights for them to show it on the news, but they didn't. When I called Rasmusson, he told me the manager of the station refused to put a story about flying saucers on the air.

"It's the strangest thing," added Uncle Myron. "You see something incredible and you know you saw it, but people either don't believe you or don't care. Well, we know what we saw, Shelley, no matter what anyone says. That's the way a lot of other people who have seen flying saucers must feel, too." He told me he hoped we'd be visiting again next summer and then asked to say hello to my little sister.

Soon after that conversation, I found out Dad really didn't believe I'd seen a space ship. I was returning from doing my homework at Parkinson's, and just as I was about to open the back screen door, I heard Mom and Dad talking. I waited outside on the landing and listened while peeking through the kitchen window.

"It's not that I don't believe him," Dad said, as he tossed his famous Caesar salad at the sink. "It's just that the astronomer could be right—they might have been mistaken."

"I don't think so," said Mom, as she stuck a fork into her bubbling cheese casserole, "because both of them saw it."

"Okay," said Dad, "let's say they really saw a flying saucer. The problem is, it's becoming an obsession with Shelley. He seems more interested in writing letters about it to people than in his schoolwork. The next thing he'll do is go to Channel Two News, and we'll have a minicam right in our living room! Since he has no concrete proof, he's just going to be laughed at or—"

Just then my father spotted me, so I walked into the kitchen. "Don't you realize Uncle Myron and I saw a space ship from another *world*?" I asked my parents. "And I don't understand why you don't want me to tell people the truth, Dad. You always told me to fight for what I think is right."

Dad looked really embarrassed as he sat down on a kitchen chair. "Shelley," he said, "I hate to tell you this, but it's possible that you and Uncle Myron were mistaken. You remember that time we saw *Poltergeist* and you thought things were moving around in your room?"

"But I was just a little kid then! I can't believe you don't believe me, Dad," I said, really shaken.

"It's not that I don't believe you, Shelley," answered Dad. "People can be mistaken for a variety of reasons. Do you realize that if you're right about the flying saucer, we're actually being visited by aliens from outer space? I think it's more likely that you saw an airplane playing a trick or something of that nature."

"You're the one who's supposed to stick up for me against the rest of the world, and you're telling me I saw an airplane!" I yelled, just as Jane came into the room to see what was going on. I was so disgusted and hurt that I ran to my room and refused to come out for dinner.

At about seven o'clock there was a knock on my door, and Jane asked, "Shelley, can I come in?"

I carefully unlocked my door so that only my little sister

could get in. She sat down on my bed, where I was writing my report about the Babylonians or the Sumerians, I forget which. "I'll always believe you, Shelley," Jane said. "Here's a friendship necklace," she added, handing me a gigantic beaded necklace she'd made. "You're not going to run away, are you?" she asked worriedly.

"What?"

"I saw a TV show about teenagers who fight with their parents and then run away, and you're thirteen and a half."

"No, I'm not going to run away, Morrie," I said, patting the kid on the head. I came out of the room and ate some of Mom's cold casserole.

That night I thought about the UFO situation. I'd gotten nowhere telling the story, and now my parents and even my sister were worried about me. There was something else that made the whole thing pretty impossible. Uncle Myron and I didn't have a shred of what the astronomer and Dad had called "concrete proof," which meant that there was no way for us to separate ourselves from the people who make up stories about flying saucers and other weird stuff just to get attention. I mean, let's say you went outside tonight and really saw Big Foot. If you had no proof, how in the world could you convince people that what you saw was real?

I added all these reasons together and saw that it was useless to keep carrying on about the UFO. I decided that except for Uncle Myron, I would keep it to myself when I was with other people.

After I'd kept quiet about the UFO for a month or so, it

more or less got forgotten. Oh, now and then a kid in the lunchroom would throw a paper airplane in my direction and say, "Look out! Flying saucer!"—but that didn't happen very often. Near the beginning of second semester, Mr. Munk asked us to write a *fictional* story, and I wrote a longer version of my first paper, explaining about the UFO. He gave me an A– and wrote, "This shows terrific imagination!"

There was a girl in my Latin class who I often saw after school at McDonald's. In March I asked her to go to a movie with me. The movie was pretty good, and afterwards we went over to the game arcade at the Seven-Eleven on Roscoe Street. But I kept comparing her to Trish Vincent.

In late March George Parkinson and I both tried out for the freshman baseball team. Park made it and I didn't, but I had a lot of fun anyway playing intramural softball. In June three of my cartoons made it into *Harkenings*—the high school yearbook. I wound up with two As and two Bs, including an A from Mr. Munk.

After school let out, Mom and Dad told us that we were going to spend even more time in Copper Creek than we had the summer before. Dad had found a publisher for his book, and Mom had gotten what she called a "firm commitment" from a small publisher in Des Moines, Iowa. The problem was that Dad had to cut *Virgil for Kids* from eight hundred to two hundred pages and Mom had to write a bunch more poems because her editor liked only a third of them. I could hardly wait to get back to the resort, because I was looking forward to seeing Uncle Myron and I had plans to try a new start with Trish Vincent. Also, in the back of my mind, I wondered if I might spot another flying saucer up there.

Because we were going to be spending two months at the resort, Mom and Dad said I could ask George Parkinson to join us for a week or so and Jane could ask her best friend, Cynthia Fender. It turned out that Cynthia could spend the first couple weeks of the vacation with us, but George couldn't make it because he was going to summer school. On a lovely June dawn, we left Chicago with Cynthia Fender and Jane sitting in Calamity's backseat and me sitting by myself in the tail section. By sunset—after two meal stops and about five bathroom stops for Jane and Cynthia—we were 450 miles north of home in Copper Creek, Michigan.

6

Too Good To Be True

I have a funny reaction to people. Some I see almost every day of my life, yet I feel like I don't know them at all. Others I consider close friends even though I've only spent a little time with them. Uncle Myron belonged to the second group. When he came out of the office with Randa on that June afternoon, I felt as if I were greeting a lifelong friend.

Uncle Myron gave us the key to Cottage Ten, and *boy* did that bed feel great after the long ride! We all hit the sack right away. (Jane didn't need for me to sleep with her because she had Cynthia Fender.) When we awoke in the morning, we unpacked. When we finished, Dad said, "Let's take Uncle Myron to that great diner in Odell for breakfast."

While Dad drove to Odell, Uncle Myron filled the folks in on the past year's events, but I didn't listen because my mind was on Trish. "What if she's moved back to Detroit?" I asked myself. "Or what if she still hates me?" By the time Dad parked the wagon on Iron Street, my heart was thumping wildly.

I let everyone walk into the diner ahead of me, and then

I went up to the window and looked in. I couldn't see for a while because it was dark inside compared to the bright summer light outside, but when my eyes cleared I saw her smiling and handing a menu to Jane. When Trish glanced outside, I felt happier than I could ever remember because I knew she was looking for me. It was then that I walked in and quietly sat down.

Everyone else ordered bacon and eggs. When my turn came, I looked up at Trish's face for a second. Her braces were gone and she had a few pimples, but they kind of blended in with her lovely red hair and freckles. "Cherry Coke, please—and an order of french fries," I told Trish. Dad looked at me and said, "For *breakfast?*" When Trish smiled while writing my order, my heart fluttered in excitement because I could tell I'd be able to make a fresh start with her.

After breakfast, Uncle Myron and Cynthia Fender helped us shop at the Big Dollar while Dad went to the Odell Carnegie Library to stock up on books. On the way back to the resort, Uncle Myron said, "The new downtown I was telling you about is right up this road."

I looked up to see a sign that said DOWNTOWN COPPER CREEK with an arrow pointing up the dirt road. "Downtown Copper Creek?" I asked. "I thought it was abandoned."

"Didn't you hear Uncle Myron tell us at the restaurant about the religious group that moved into town and fixed it up?" asked Mom.

I'd been paying attention to Trish Vincent at the restaurant, and I hadn't heard a word any of them had said. "Religious group?" I repeated to Uncle Myron.

Turning around from the front seat, my uncle said, "Some people bought the land from the mining company. They're a religious group that came from Virginia just a couple weeks ago—maybe fifty of them or so. They're turning Copper Creek back into a regular town—stores, houses, and everything. I've been there two or three times to get some things, and they're pleasant as can be. You'd be amazed at what they've done to the town," he added, as we pulled onto the resort's gravel driveway.

After I helped Mom and Dad put the groceries away, I walked over to the office. "Come in," Uncle Myron called from his room.

I sat on his bed, and we talked about what we both had done the past year. He showed me the paintings he had done, and I asked about Nathan, the raccoon, because I hadn't seen him around the cottages. Uncle Myron explained that Nathan had started spending more and more time out in the wild, and then one spring day hadn't come back. I told him about my grades and how I'd had three cartoons in *Harkenings*. Then we started talking about the UFO and how nobody had realized the significance of what we'd seen.

"I give you credit for writing all those letters," Uncle Myron told me. "At first I was really burned up when Chief McMaster and the newspaper editor and the TV station and everyone you wrote to didn't believe us, but then I started thinking. You trust your mom and dad, don't you?"

"More or less."

"But what if your dad said he saw a pink elephant floating over his car on his way home from work? Would you believe him?"

"A pink elephant?" I repeated.

"Well, that's the way people are about this. Harv Holmquist has seen strange lights in the sky several times, but even he looked at me funny when I told him about it. If you claim to have experienced something far enough out of the ordinary, not even your own brother will believe you."

"My sister believes me."

He smiled and said, "I decided to drop it, Shelley—not from my mind, but from talking about it with other people. No one can ever convince me we didn't see a space ship, but what's the use in banging your head against a brick wall?"

"That's exactly what I figured."

Uncle Myron put his big tattooed arm around my shoulder and added, "I missed you this winter, Shelley." Before I left his room, he told me he'd gotten a special filter for the telescope so that we could observe the sun and that he'd found some places down the stream where there were fossils.

Mom and Dad had brought along a tiny portable TV, which we set up in Cottage One, right where Uncle Myron's TV had been stolen the year before. The second morning of our vacation, Jane and Cynthia and I were in Cottage One watching cartoons when Dad came in and said, "I've got to go into town to get something. Anybody want to come along?"

Jane and Cynthia were busy playing Barbies while they

watched, but I said, "Sure," because I figured we'd go to Odell.

Dad and I had driven maybe two miles on Highway 2 when we saw a wooden sign with DOWNTOWN COPPER CREEK on it and the arrow pointing up the dirt road. Just a few feet up the road was a bigger sign that listed about half a dozen stores, including Davis Grocery, Coe Appliances, Cregar Shoes, and Del Monaco's Restaurant.

"Maybe I can get what I need in downtown Copper Creek and save a twelve-mile drive," Dad said, veering off onto the dirt road with a squeal of the wagon's wheels.

As Dad explained that the dirt was greenish blue from the copper in it, I was observing the amazing changes that had occurred since I had seen the Copper Creek downtown the year before. A couple hundred yards up the dirt road I could see a bunch of new stores where the old, abandoned ghost town had stood. At the outskirts of downtown, a cluster of houses was nearing completion and a crew was paving the road.

We parked the wagon on the side of the dirt road about a hundred feet in front of where the paving crew was working. As we walked past them, the crew smiled and waved and a man sitting on the big yellow paving machine said, "Howdy, fellas." "Howdy," Dad responded, with a tip of his Budweiser hat. Once we'd passed the crew, I glanced over my shoulder to see if they were snickering at us. They were still standing there smiling, and the guy on the paving machine waved again.

The newly paved road was blocked off by orange cones,

so we had to walk on the edges of the front lawns while passing the new houses. There were twelve of them—six on each side of the street. They were large, pretty houses, and they all looked the same except for three things. Half were made of yellow brick, while the other half were made of orange. The shrubs and trees on the long green lawns were different from house to house. And, each house had a different-colored roof.

Up on those rooftops, workmen were hammering down shingles and putting up TV antennas. One of them called, "Hello," and another, "How're you?" and Dad called, "Fine, how're you?" and tipped his hat to them.

"Nice people, aren't they, chum?" Dad asked, as we passed a new, green OAK AVENUE sign.

"Yeah," I answered, thinking how strange it was that they were so friendly.

Just beyond the houses we came to a white church. It looked like your typical small-town white wooden church, only it was at least four times as big. A sign on the broad lawn in front of the church said COPPER CREEK UNIVERSAL HUMANIST CHURCH. A man high up on a ladder was dipping his paintbrush into a bucket of white paint as we passed.

"Any spots I missed?" he cheerfully asked.

We both looked up at the white steeple, which was beautiful against the deep blue sky. After studying it for a few seconds, Dad made his thumb and index finger into an **O** and said, "Looks fine."

Just beyond the church, Oak Avenue crossed the main

downtown street, Copper Street, where there were a number of new and nearly finished buildings, including a restaurant, a grocery, an appliance store, and a couple little shops. Have you ever seen a Western movie in which the pioneers are happily building a town? That's the way it was in Copper Creek. Men, women, and children were sawing, hammering, painting, and stacking things on shelves. Everyone who saw us smiled and said, "Hello." Dad returned their friendliness, but I didn't. I live in Chicago, and people there aren't friendly at all. In fact, if someone comes up to you and says "Hi," you get suspicious that he's going to mug you or try to sell you drugs.

"Maybe we can get what I need here," Dad said, pointing to the DAVIS GROCERY sign that was swinging in the summer breeze. Inside the store, a redheaded, teenaged boy was taping hand-printed signs in the window advertising shaving cream, fruit drinks, and other items. A man and woman were taking cans of food out of boxes and putting them on shelves.

Dad walked to the row of medicines. "Good, they have it," he said, taking a hemorrhoid ointment off the shelf.

"Did you find what you needed?" asked the grocer, following us to the checkout counter. "I'm Mr. Davis, and that's my wife." He gestured toward the woman opening boxes.

"Pleased to meet you," Dad said, and he introduced himself and me. While the grocer rang up the sale, I looked at his moustache, his oval head with a bald spot on top, his glasses, and his white apron, and I knew I knew him from somewhere.

"Where're you folks from?" Mr. Davis asked, as he handed Dad his change.

"Chicago," Dad answered.

"How's the weather up there?" his wife asked. There was something about her that was also strangely familiar.

"Pretty good," Dad answered.

"Glad to have you folks stop by our little town," Mr. Davis said. When he looked at me and said, "Take a mint, son, they're on the house," I nearly thought of who he reminded me of. I kept trying to think of it as we walked back to the car.

When we reached Highway 2, I said to Dad, "Wasn't there something weird about those people?"

"What do you mean?"

"People just—they're just not that nice."

"It's just our big-city background, chum. Don't you think it's weirder to think people are weird just *because* they're nice?"

"That lady asked how the weather is *up* in Chicago. Don't you think *that's* weird?"

"Shelley, lots of people don't know directions, especially if they've just moved from far away."

Once at the resort, I went over to Uncle Myron, who was standing in his brown shorts at his easel just outside the office. "Dad and I went to downtown Copper Creek," I said.

He looked up from the painting of Indianface Mountain he was doing. "Oh?"

"You said you've been there a couple times, right?"

"Right."

"Well?"

"What?" he asked, wiping the sweat from his face with the clean end of a paint-stained cloth.

"Don't you think everyone there is just too—too nice and friendly?"

"You're thinking that they might not be from this planet, aren't you?" After I nodded, Uncle Myron said, "I started thinking a little like that myself when I first met them. Then I realized that if we hadn't seen that thing, I'd just assume they were nice people. Shelley, people who settle in a new place *have* to be nice to get along."

I decided that maybe Dad and Uncle Myron were right—it wasn't fair to jump to conclusions or hold it against people for being friendly. But I still wondered why the grocer and his wife had seemed so familiar.

One bad part about the new town in Copper Creek was that it meant we'd be going to Odell less often. Odell was twelve miles from the resort and downtown Copper Creek was just two miles away. Mom and Dad figured that even if the Davis Grocery was a bit more expensive, it was worth the savings in gas to do some of our shopping there.

We'd been on vacation for a few days when the folks asked Jane, Cynthia, and me if we wanted to go shopping with them in Copper Creek. Jane and Cynthia stayed at the resort to play with some paints Uncle Myron had given us. But I wanted to observe the Copper Creekers again.

The roads in Copper Creek were all paved now, so Dad drove Calamity right onto Copper Street and parked her in front of the Davis Grocery. "Meet you here later," I said, as

Mom and Dad walked into the store. "I'm going to walk around."

The redheaded kid was outside the grocery sweeping the new white sidewalk with a broom. He had an old-fashioned crew cut and an open, wide-eyed expression—a real all-American-type kid. As I looked at the cowlick of red hair that stuck up from one point of his head, it struck me that there was something familiar about him, too. This time it came to me. He looked more than a little like Richie Cunningham on the show "Happy Days."

"Hi," I said, with a big smile. "I should have introduced myself last time. Shelley Virgil Monahan."

He shook my hand and said, "Bob Davis is my name—glad to meet ya." His voice wasn't at all like Richie's.

We stared at each other self-consciously for a few seconds, and then he asked eagerly, "I was wondering, Shelley—how do you get your teeth so white?"

"What?"

"If it's not too personal, Shelley, I was wondering which brand of toothpaste you use."

I answered that strange question. Then I said, "Glad to meet you, Bob—see you around."

I walked around Copper Creek and saw that a lot more work had been done on the new town in the few days since I'd first been there. I went into the hardware store to see if they had any Wiffle balls and bats, but they didn't, and then I passed Cregar Shoes, where a short man with white bushy eyebrows was fitting a woman with shoes. Several of the people I saw on my walk looked or sounded familiar. I decided that the best way to figure out why was to observe them in a friendly manner, so I smiled and said "Hello" to everyone I passed.

Next door to Del Monaco's Restaurant—and just two doors down from the Davis Grocery—was a store with COE APPLIANCES painted neatly in red, white, and blue on the window. Inside I saw two men unloading crates. Since there were several TVs turned on in the store, I thought I'd go in and watch a little tube while the folks finished their shopping.

I tried the door, but it was locked. However, the older man inside saw me, came to the door, and opened it.

"Hello, young man," he said. He was a tall guy who looked about thirty or so. He had jet black hair, perfect white teeth, and the big smile that everyone in town seemed to have.

"I thought you were open," I said, glancing at the TVs.

"We're planning on opening in a few days. But you can come in and watch. The name's Rob Coe."

"Shelley Monahan," I said, holding out my hand to shake his. Still smiling at him, I asked, "Have we ever met before? You look familiar."

"I don't believe so," he answered.

The young man who had been unloading crates with Mr. Coe came over to introduce himself. "Hey, glad to meet ya. Dwayne's the name—Dwayne Coe," he said, shaking my hand so hard it hurt. Dwayne was about nineteen years old, I figured. He was taller and broader than his father, and he had brown freckles high up on his cheeks, but he had the same black hair and perfect white teeth as Mr. Coe. It struck me that Dwayne looked a little like the Fonz on the show "Happy Days," but he didn't sound like the Fonz.

"Have a seat and watch TV as long as you want, Shelley," Mr. Coe offered.

"Thanks," I said, and sat down in a chair in front of a TV. While Mr. Coe and Dwayne unloaded TVs and carried them into a back room, I watched the Partridge family solve another of its problems.

By the next commercial, Mr. Coe was doing some paperwork and making calls at his desk and Dwayne had left the store. While a pimple medicine ad was being shown on TV, Mr. Coe said, "I've got a daughter just about your age." He looked outside and added, "That's a coincidence. Here's Marsha now."

The bell on the door tinkled, and in walked a beautiful blonde girl. She had gorgeous blue eyes, which grew larger as she looked at me shyly and said, "Hi."

For a second it seemed to me that she looked a little like a TV character I couldn't quite place, but as she smiled at me I told myself, "Shelley Virgil Monahan, you're going *nuts!*" Remembering my manners, I then introduced myself to Marsha Coe.

While Marsha helped her dad with his paperwork, I watched the rest of the show. It made me feel stupid to watch TV while she filed things, so when the next commercial came on, I asked, "You live in this town?"

"Eight Oak Avenue. The house with the blue roof," she said, with a cheerful, musical laugh.

While Marsha filed, she asked me where we were staying

and where we were from and what my hobbies were and things like that. We were still talking when her dad said he wanted her to put price tags on some appliances in the back room.

"You can come with me if you want," she said, walking away. Boy, was she beautiful! As I followed her, my legs were kind of quaking with excitement because girls as pretty as Marsha usually didn't even look my way.

The back room was piled with TVs, radios, toaster ovens, and such. Marsha gave me a red Magic Marker, and I wrote the prices on the tags while she read the numbers from a clipboard. I asked her where she went to school, and she informed me that the Copper Creek kids would be going to school in Odell the following autumn. We talked about our favorite TV shows and about how there wasn't much to do around there, and then I heard familiar voices from the front of the store.

"Here he is," said Mr. Coe, bringing my parents into the back room. "I'm afraid Marsha put him to work."

"That's amazing—I can't even get him to dry the dishes," said Mom. She and Dad each had two grocery bags in their hands.

"This is my daughter, Marsha," said Mr. Coe. He then introduced her to everyone.

"Well, I guess I've got to go. Nice meeting you," I said to Marsha. "You, too, Mr. Coe."

I felt thrilled all the way back to the resort. From having no girls in my life except for the one date with the girl in my Latin class, I now *almost* had two. There was Trish Vincent, who I liked and who maybe liked me. And there was Marsha Coe, who obviously liked me and who was so beautiful. As I went to my room to begin a drawing of her, I told myself, "Maybe she never gets to see any boys, so that's why she likes me." See, I suspected that there was something strange about the Copper Creekers, but Marsha made me want to kid myself that I was just imagining it.

That evening there was an unusual event in the sky. Uncle Myron explained that the moon was "occulting" a star, meaning it was moving in front of the star. He invited Harv and Betty Holmquist and all us Monahans and Cynthia Fender out to watch it. While we were waiting at the telescope for the moon to occult the star, the phone rang in the office.

A few seconds later, my uncle returned and said, "It's for you, Shelley."

"Me?"

I went inside the office and picked up the phone. "Hello, Shelley?" said a soft voice. "It's me—Marsha."

"Oh. Hi."

"Hi. I wanted to ask you if you could come over for dinner tomorrow. Could you?"

"Dinner? Sure. Sure I could."

"About six o'clock? See you tomorrow?"

"Tomorrow," I said.

As I walked back outside, I heard Uncle Myron shout that I should come quick, the moon was just grazing the edge of the star. I missed it, but I didn't care. A beautiful blonde girl had asked *me*, Shelley Virgil Monahan, over for dinner at her house, and I'd just met her. I really don't remember walking back to the group. I think I probably floated out to them.

"Who was that?" Dad asked.

"I'm invited somewhere tomorrow night—in Copper Creek. Over to the Coes' house for dinner."

"Oh," Dad said, looking at Mom.

Jane giggled and whispered something in Cynthia's ear, and then Cynthia giggled.

We looked at some galaxies and double stars. Harv Holmquist drank so much of his blackberry wine that he nearly toppled the telescope when it was his turn to look through it. When his wife whispered something to him, he snapped: "I am *not* drunk, Betty. It's how I relax after a hard day." Shortly after that the Holmquists left, Uncle Myron put the telescope away, and we all went inside.

For the first time in nearly a year, I didn't think of Trish Vincent as I went to sleep. I thought of Marsha Coe.

7

Marsha Coe

The next afternoon while I paced around the cottage thinking about my date with Marsha Coe, Dad asked, "Want me to drive you tonight, chum?"

I didn't want my dad to drive me to the second date of my life, so I answered, "No thanks, it's only a couple miles and I can walk."

"Wait a second," Mom said. "I think Uncle Myron has an old bicycle you might be able to borrow."

Inside the little utility room where he kept his refrigerator, stove, and other appliances, Uncle Myron had an old, rusty Schwinn. It looked like it had been propped up against the wall in back of the clothes washer for a decade. "Borrow it—you can *have* it," Uncle Myron said. I knocked the cobwebs off the bike and rode it around the gravel driveway to see how it worked. It was hard to push the pedals and the bike squeaked a lot, but Uncle Myron had an oilcan and a screwdriver in his utility room, and those problems were soon pretty well solved. I decided that later on I'd sand and repaint the bike, fill the tires with air, and get a light for it.

But even as it was now, the red Schwinn was a decent means of transportation.

I wore a nice shirt and slacks for my date with Marsha. I even took Dad's razor and shaving cream out of the medicine cabinet and shaved my upper lip. See, I have these few hairs that kind of grow there—a moustache, I guess you might call them—and I wanted to get rid of them for the date.

At about 5:30 I got on the bike and began pedalling toward downtown Copper Creek. Marsha, wearing a bright yellow dress, came to the door at Eight Oak Avenue to answer my ring. At Lakeside High the girls rarely wear dresses even on dates—they wear jeans like the guys. To think that this beautiful girl had dressed up like this for me almost caused me to faint.

Marsha's dad sat in his easy chair watching the news and saying, "How terrible! How terrible!" while Mrs. Coe prepared dinner. As we sat on the couch eating little appetizers that her mom had made, Marsha asked me all kinds of questions about school, my friends in Chicago, and so on. No one had *ever* seemed so interested in me. Through the doorway to the kitchen, I could see Mrs. Coe scurrying about as she said things like "I hope I don't burn the rice." From time to time Mr. Coe looked away from the news and smiled at Marsha and me.

At 6:30, Mrs. Coe placed a platter of roast beef on the table and said, "You three wash your hands, and please call Dwayne to the table, Marsha."

"Gee, come on, Marsh, the baseball game just started," I

heard Dwayne say from a bedroom as I washed my hands. He didn't come to the table until after Mr. Coe went to get him.

During *my* family's meals, Mom jots down notes on napkins, Dad lectures us about the history of tomatoes, and Jane and I make faces and occasionally throw green beans or peas at each other. When I want something I say, "Pass that stuff, Morrie." The Coes were as polite as could be. "Please pass the roast beef," and, "Would you pass the salad?" they said to each other.

"Everything's great," I said, as I ate my roast beef.

Mrs. Coe smiled proudly and said, "Thank you, Shelley."

Then, to make conversation, I said, "Mr. Coe, you look much too young to have a son Dwayne's age—and so does Mrs. Coe."

I hoped they'd take that as a compliment, but Mr. Coe gave Mrs. Coe a concerned look and said, "Really?" Then he composed himself, smiled and said, "Well, Mary and I married early."

To change the subject, I asked, "What's the name of your organization?"

"Organization?" Mr. Coe echoed.

"Religious group, I mean."

He turned serious and answered, "We're called the Universal Humanists, Shelley. We believe that kindness toward one's fellow human beings and a pleasant life for everyone are the most important things in the world."

When I said, "That sounds wonderful," he looked

pleased, and as he smiled he reminded me very much of someone I knew. I felt that I was about to think of who when Dwayne said, "Mom, can I have another helping of corn? It's nibblin' good." As he heaped more corn onto his plate, I looked to see if he was joking because his words were almost exactly those of a TV advertisement for canned corn, but he appeared serious. They're weird, I thought as I finished dinner, but there's something pleasant about them, and they're from some other state, and here's this beautiful girl sitting next to me and staring at me like that, so why worry about it?

After dinner Marsha took me into her room and showed me her coin collection. As I sat on her bed looking at her coins, I suddenly burst into laughter. All her coins were from 1983, 1984, and 1985.

"What's so funny?" Marsha cheerfully asked.

"Your collection. You've got ten 1983 coins, about two dozen 1984 ones, and dozens from 1985."

Looking hurt, she asked: "What's wrong with that?"

"Nothing, it's just that most people have coins from all different years in their collections."

"I like the shiny new ones, Shelley," she said, and I could see the tears beginning to overflow her eyes.

"Oh, it's a beautiful collection Marsha—just a little unusual."

It was just my luck that Dad drove up to get me right then. It turned out that Mom and Dad didn't want me to ride home late at night without a light. When we heard Dad's voice, Marsha and I went into the living room.

"Do you have a few minutes?" Mrs. Coe asked Dad. "I have dessert. Baked it myself."

Dad took off his Chicago Bulls jacket and sat down while Marsha went next door to ask the Cregars to join us. "Nils Cregar's mayor of the town," Mr. Coe explained to Dad. "He owns a shoe store just a few doors away from my store."

A couple minutes later Marsha returned with a short, gray-haired man who had white, bushy eyebrows. "Edna couldn't come, but I make it a practice to never pass up free desserts or extra income tax deductions," Mr. Cregar said. "Glad to meet you, Shelley," he told me, after we were introduced. "You walked past my store yesterday, didn't you? I never forget a pair of feet."

Dessert was peach pie with whipped cream on top. While we ate it, Mr. Coe asked Dad what he did for a living.

"I'm a professor of Classics at Stevenson College in Chicago," Dad answered.

"Oh, *classics*!" Mrs. Coe said excitedly. "I love the great old songs."

Dad held his spoon in midair and stared at her. "No, classical Latin and Greek literature, I meant," he explained.

"Oh—of course," Mrs. Coe said.

Mr. Cregar, who had been quiet during dessert, suddenly said, "I heard a couple good ones the other day." He then told three or four jokes. After one of them, Dad laughed so hard that he choked.

"You rattle those off like Johnny Carson," Dad said.

That caught my attention, but I didn't know whether or

not Mayor Cregar told jokes like Johnny Carson because I'd never watched the "Tonight Show."

"Johnny Carson? Really? Thanks," the mayor said, but he seemed a bit worried. "I've got an even better one. What time is it when an elephant sits on your fence?"

I'm sure you've heard the standard answer to that old one. I figured he had some clever twist, but when Dad said, "I give up," Nils answered: "Time to get a new fence!"

The Coes roared, but Dad and I just managed weak smiles. We finished the pie, and then Dad and I thanked them, put on our jackets, and went to the door. "Well, I'll be seeing you," I said to Marsha.

Making her blue eyes very large, she softly said, "I'll be looking forward to it, Shelley."

As Dad and I put the bicycle into the back of Calamity, he said, "You were right, chum, there *is* something peculiar about them," but I wasn't paying much attention to him.

As I think over all the things Marsha and the others said and did that night, I wonder how I could have ever kidded myself about them being regular people. All I can say is, I very badly *wanted* to believe that they were regular folks because of Marsha, and so for a while I kind of told myself that they were.

The next day I phoned Marsha from Uncle Myron's room and asked her out on a date for Monday night. They were showing *E.T.* at the Odell Theatre. Marsha said she hadn't seen it and would love to go with me.

Dad agreed to take us to the movie and pick us up. Like I said before, it makes you feel funny to have your dad drive you on a date. But I was only fourteen years old at the time, and it was twelve miles to Odell, so what could I do?

Marsha was as bright, cheerful, and lovely as usual when we picked her up on that night in late June. She had on another beautiful dress—an old-fashioned pink one.

Dad took us to the early show at the Odell Theatre—the 5:05 one—because it cost only two dollars apiece to get in then, and I was using my own money. He let us off and then went to the library while we went to the movie. Just as Marsha and I were going into the theater, Trish Vincent came out of the diner down the street. On the way to her apartment, she glanced our way. I've got to admit I was glad she saw me with Marsha. I hoped seeing me with another girl would make her jealous.

I'd seen *E.T.* twice before. Marsha took the movie incredibly seriously, which was nice for me. During all the scary and sad scenes, she reached out and took my hand. When she did that, I'd look over and see her big blue eyes staring at the screen, that great blonde hair of hers, and her pretty knees, which were visible just below her pink dress. I felt as if I was melting like the butter they put on the popcorn when I had her hand in mine.

In the scene where they think E.T. is dead, she actually started to cry. She cried so loudly people in the audience stared at her, and when I said, "Marsha, shhhhh!" she said, "I can't help it." Then, when E.T. came back to life, she laughed loudly through tears of joy, and people again stared.

After the movie ended, we were walking up the aisle over

the crunched popcorn when Marsha said something astounding: "I'm glad they showed it without commercials, aren't you, Shelley?"

"Yeah," I said, and then suddenly a bulb lit up in my head. "What do you mean, without commercials?"

"Oh, don't they usually have commercials during movies?"

I stared at her smiling face and thought about that question and about some of the other things she had said and done. "No," I answered, "but sometimes before movies they show ads, and they're sort of like commercials."

Dad met us outside the theater and drove us to Copper Creek. I walked Marsha inside her house, and as we stood in the hallway she said, "I really enjoyed tonight, Shelley." When she looked at me with her blue eyes, I felt myself starting to melt again, but her words about the commercials were still echoing in my mind. "We'll have to do it again," I answered, and managed a smile.

I do a lot of my best thinking in bed. That night I told my folks I was tired and went to bed early—about 10:00—so that I could think about all the strange things the Copper Creekers had said and done. There had been lots of little things, such as their unusual friendliness and politeness, Marsha's coin collection, and Marsha's thinking that movies at theaters had commercials. There was also the way so many of them seemed familiar or resembled people on TV.

On the other hand, I've had experiences where being suspicious has made me do really dumb things. I remember one time when I enrolled in a day camp in the middle of the session and I was sure the other kids wouldn't like me. The first day I saw some kids pointing at me and saying what I thought was "Jew," and I almost got into a fight over it. It turned out that they were saying, "He's new," and were perfectly nice kids. In the case of Marsha's people, I had been suspicious as soon as I had heard that there were new people in Copper Creek. Maybe I had looked so closely at them that I had imagined they were aliens. And as for the weird little things they said, maybe the Copper Creekers had stayed away from daily life because of their religion and just didn't know about a lot of stuff.

The problem was, How could I find out the truth about them? There was only one way I could think of. I had to observe them when they didn't know I was watching. I decided to spy on the Copper Creekers that very night.

8

They're Aliens!

My parents stayed up past midnight, so it was no easy trick to get out of there without being noticed. I shut and locked the door of my room, got dressed, and then opened the sliding windows. As quietly as I could, I climbed from my bed and over the windowsill. I went out the window head first and tumbled down onto the gravel.

Fortunately, the moon was low in the west, so I could see a little. But it was cold out, and the air was so wet with dew I could feel it in my lungs when I breathed.

I decided it was safer to walk the two miles than to ride them on the Schwinn. I walked up the gravel driveway to the road and headed toward downtown Copper Creek.

Despite the moon, it was pretty dark. The sunflowers that seemed so bright and cheery during the day looked like heads leaning toward me on both sides of Copper Creek Road. The forest beyond was totally dark and swayed in the breeze like an army of giants. Wherever I passed, the crickets stopped their chirping, and there was something eerie about that sudden silence.

I was only a few hundred feet from the resort when something swooped down very close to my head. I ducked, wheeled around, and began running back. Probably I would have banged on the door and screamed for Mom and Dad to let me in if I hadn't seen the flying object flitting away against the face of the moon. It was one of the small brown bats that are all over the place up there.

I did not see a single car on Highway 2 as I walked eastward along the gravel shoulder. After about twenty minutes I came to the DOWNTOWN COPPER CREEK sign. As I approached the two rows of houses on Oak Avenue, I could see the glow of TV sets in most of the living rooms.

I crept up to the Coes' house. From behind an evergreen, I spied on them through their picture window. The entire family—Mr. and Mrs. Coe and Marsha and Dwayne—were sitting in front of the TV.

They were watching a rerun of "Laverne and Shirley." In case any of you are reading this in the year 2000, "Laverne and Shirley" was a show about a couple of plain-looking but funny girls who worked in a Milwaukee beer factory and were always trying to meet men.

I couldn't hear the Coes talking from in front of the house. But on the side of the house I found a window that was partway open just behind the couch where they were sitting. I knelt down behind that window so that only my eyes and the top of my head were visible. Then I watched and listened.

The Coes laughed along with the laughter on the sound track. They actually *laughed*. Nothing against "Laverne and

Shirley," but most people watching TV barely chuckle even at the funniest scenes.

A commercial came on and Marsha said to her folks: "I made a mistake tonight. I said something about there not being commercials during the movie, and he looked at me funny."

"We've been over that, Marsha, dear," said Mrs. Coe. "If you don't know about something, you shouldn't talk about it. You've never been to a movie in a theater before."

"Oh, I'm sure she did just fine, Mary," Mr. Coe said. "Besides, Shelley's so crazy about Marsha, I doubt he'd notice her mistakes."

"Hey!" Dwayne said. "How about you thinking Classics meant old songs, Mom?" While he watched TV, Dwayne was punching in the pocket of the baseball glove he had on his left hand.

Mrs. Coe nodded and said, "I still feel just terrible about that one. When they say 'classics' on TV, they usually mean old songs."

"I'm not sure we can learn everything about them from TV," said Marsha. "Maybe we should spend more time on newspapers and books."

"Hey, I don't need any more *books*!" said Dwayne, and I realized that he even had the Fonz's facial expression when he said that.

"If you don't learn to read better, you're really going to stand out when you go to Odell High this fall," said Marsha.

"Say, listen, Sis, from what I hear there's lots of teenagers that can't read. Besides, I've learned to read all right from 'Sesame Street' and whatayacallit—'Electric Company.'"

Mr. Coe laughed happily and said, "That Laverne sure is something, isn't she?" Then he dreamily added, "Maybe you're right about the books, Marsha, but I don't think they're *that* important."

The show ended and Mr. Coe got up to switch the channel. As he walked back to the couch, I quickly ducked down so that he wouldn't spot me. I could hear a commercial for a hair dye on TV.

"Dear," Mrs. Coe said to her husband, "I believe Shelley was right. You *do* look too young to have a son Dwayne's age. I think you should make yourself a little older."

"I think you're right, Mary," Mr. Coe said. "Wait a second, I'll give it a try now as long as the commercial's on." I picked up my head to watch. As he closed his eyes, I realized that Mr. Coe had more than a slight resemblance to Mr. Brady, the father in "The Brady Bunch," although his voice didn't sound at all like Mr. Brady's.

My thoughts were interrupted by a shocking sight. As Mr. Coe sat concentrating with his eyes closed, wrinkles slowly appeared around his eyes and his hair developed streaks of gray.

"No—way too much, Dad," Marsha said.

"Hey, you're supposed to be our dad—not our grand-dad," Dwayne said.

The show came back on and Mr. Coe said, "Oh, well, I'll fool around with it while I'm shaving tomorrow."

"Just a trace of gray and a couple wrinkles would make

you look nice and dignified, dear," said Mrs. Coe. Like the final pieces in a jigsaw puzzle, the pieces of the Coes fell in place. With her beehive hairdo and long, checked, old-fashioned dress, Mrs. Coe looked a lot like Marian Cunningham—the mother on "Happy Days." She had the same absentminded, innocent, little-girl personality as Mrs. Cunningham, too. What had thrown me off was the fact that the Coes didn't have the voices of the TV characters they resembled. For example, although Dwayne looked like the Fonz, he talked a little like the older brother, Wally, on "Leave It to Beaver." Marsha looked like the youngest sister in "The Brady Bunch," but her voice sounded like Jeannie's in "I Dream of Jeannie."

Since these aliens obviously could control how they looked and sounded, I wondered what they were like in their true form. Did they look human at all, or would they seem like monsters to us?

I was so stunned by what I'd heard and seen that I had picked my head up too high above the windowsill. Marsha seemed to sense that I was there because she suddenly turned around, cupped her eyes with her hand, and peered outside. I hit the dirt instantly, then crawled as close to the house as possible. I could see Marsha standing at the window, with the light forming a kind of halo around her head as she looked outside. I waited until she sat back down on the couch. Then I crawled out of range of the window and stood up behind a newly planted tree. As I started back to the resort, my heart was pounding, my legs were trembling, and I felt cold chills throughout my body.

The moon had set, and except for the glitter of the millions of stars and the glow of the Copper Creek lights behind me, it was totally dark. At the place where Oak Avenue met Highway 2, I walked off the road and stumbled against a tree, hurting my knee.

I tried to stay on Highway 2 by the feel of the blacktop, but at a curve I walked off the road and felt myself falling. "Help!" I cried, as I rolled downhill and saw the stars spinning crazily around and around. When I landed I thought I was in some kind of deep pit, but when I stood up I found myself in the little ditch alongside the road. Shortly after that I spotted the glow of light from my bedroom in Cottage Ten. The light helped guide me back.

Although the thermometer outside Uncle Myron's office read forty-five degrees and I could see my breath, I was covered with sweat. I wanted to get my trembling body in bed, but I had to check something first. I quietly opened the door to Cottage One, felt my way to the TV, and flicked it on. Immediately I heard a voice very much like the one I'd heard telling jokes at the Coes' house—only when the picture came on, there was Johnny Carson talking instead of Mayor Nils Cregar.

As I sat watching TV by myself, my mind was at work. It was clear that the Copper Creekers were trying to appear to be regular folks. They were doing it by watching TV shows and imitating the way people looked and acted in them. What they were doing made sense. If I went to a different world and wanted to blend in, I'd have to find models to imitate. The best way might be to watch their TV or movies or read books about them and try to act and look like the people in them. I'd make mistakes, of course, and that's what they'd done. Marsha's coin collection was one of their small mistakes. But their biggest mistake was modelling themselves too closely after TV characters.

I was dying to tell someone right then and there what I knew, so I snapped off the TV in the middle of the TV minister's end-of-the-day sermon and left the cottage. After climbing in through my bedroom window, I quietly went into Mom and Dad's room. Mom was lying on her back with her mouth wide open. Dad had his arm around her and was snoring. I was about to wake them up and tell them about the Copper Creekers when I realized I couldn't. *I* knew the Copper Creekers were aliens, but I still didn't have any concrete proof.

I wanted to tell Uncle Myron, but I didn't want to scare him to death by waking him up in the middle of the night, so I returned to my room, ripped off my clothes, and went to bed in my underwear. I lay there a while and then checked my digital. It was 1:15. Strange thoughts go through your mind at that time of night. Sure, I was stunned to find myself dealing with aliens, but another feeling was starting to hit me almost as strongly. I felt a sense of loss. I'd really thought Marsha had liked me. Now I could see that I was just part of an experiment. Probably I was one of the first humans to get to know one of them. If Marsha could fool me, then maybe they were ready to fool others.

Fool others for what purpose? Did they want to conquer the world? Or were they nice aliens? In that case, maybe I could still see the lovely Marsha—even if in her true form she had two heads and green tentacles. Before I went to sleep, I decided that there was only one way to find out why they had come. I was going to confront Marsha with what I knew.

9

The Alien in the Fifty-Dollar Jeans

The next morning I phoned Marsha and asked her to go bike riding with me, and she said yes. At about eleven I pedalled the red Schwinn over to the Coes' house. Marsha came to the door carrying a big picnic basket. "Hi," she said, looking truly glad to see me. When I saw how beautiful she was in her designer jeans and checked shirt tied at the waist, I began to get that melting feeling again.

"Can you help me with my bike, Shelley?" she asked.

In the hallway Marsha had a brand-new Redline, which, if you don't know, is one of the fanciest bikes you can own. As I was helping her wheel it outside, Mr. Coe and another man came through the living room.

"Nice of you to stop by for brunch, Reverend—oh, Shelley, meet Reverend Smith," Mr. Coe said. "Reverend Smith, this handsome young man is my daughter's friend, Shelley Monahan."

Reverend Smith was about fifty years old and bigger than Harv Holmquist—about six five and built like a defensive tackle. His totally bald head didn't seem to have the right proportions for his body, though. It was much too small. As he gave my hand a hearty shake, I broke out into a cold sweat. I'd seen that small, bald, pink head and those watery gray eyes on the minister who'd given the TV sermon the previous night.

"Glad to meet you, young man," Reverend Smith said, with a southern accent I'd heard from a television sports announcer. "You'll have to come to one of our Sunday morning services sometime. Just let us know beforehand, Marsha, so we can be hospitable." Reverend Smith smiled as he spoke, but he didn't smile like most people. Although his mouth curved upward at the edges, his eyes retained their watery, blank expression.

"Thanks for the invitation, Reverend Smith," I said. "Nice meeting you."

"I'm heading to the store. See you later, Mary," Mr. Coe called toward the kitchen, and then he and Reverend Smith went out the door.

Marsha and I got her bike out the front door. "Where do you want to ride to?" I asked, in a friendly way so that she wouldn't suspect I was on to them.

"There's a pretty meadow a couple miles up the road."

"Lead the way."

We rode our bikes from Oak Avenue back to Highway 2 and then wheeled toward Odell. As we pedalled along side by side, I saw that the sunlight streaming through the trees turned Marsha's hair to ever-changing shades of gold. Now and then she looked over at me and smiled, and when she did my legs felt like Jell-O.

Five minutes up the highway, Marsha said, "We turn off here." We veered off onto a bumpy dirt road that ended after several hundred yards. At the place where the road ended was a low, rusty chain fence, and beyond that was a large field created when a part of the woods had been cleared.

"This is the meadow," Marsha said.

We lifted our bikes over the chain fence, walked them a short way into the meadow, and left them among some tall sunflowers. Marsha took my hand and led me through the sweet-smelling yellow, violet, and blue wildflowers. Looking at her smiling face, I felt dizzy.

There was just one tree in the meadow—a huge, gnarled old oak. Marsha took a small blanket from her picnic basket, unfolded it, and spread it beneath the tree. "It's pretty here, isn't it?" she asked, sitting down on the blanket.

My heart thudded as she took my hand and pulled me down onto the blanket. "Beautiful," I answered.

We sat there for a while, just staring at the meadow and at each other. The soft summer breeze was so sweet I could taste it. The whole thing would have been heavenly—if I hadn't been sitting there with an alien.

Marsha had made egg-salad and peanut butter and jelly sandwiches, and she'd also brought along a thermos of Hawaiian Punch. We ate and drank while talking about our upcoming school years. After we finished the picnic lunch, I said, in a voice that barely came out of my throat:

"Where did you folks come from, Marsha?"

"I thought you knew—from Virginia."

"I mean, where did you *really* come from?" I held her hand tightly and stared straight into her eyes, which were the color of the deep blue sky. "What planet?"

She tilted her head sideways and asked: "Are you all right, Shelley? Did my egg-salad sandwich make you sick?"

"I'm fine. It's no use lying, Marsha. I *know* you're not from Earth."

She let go of my hand as her smile faded into a puzzled look. "What makes you say that?"

"I spied on you last night while you watched TV. I saw your dad change his appearance, and I heard you talking. There've also been a lot of little things."

She took a fresh napkin from the basket and wiped the tears from the corners of her eyes. "It wasn't nice of you to spy on us, Shelley," she said, and then added, "What kind of little things?"

I explained to her about the various little mistakes. "There's something more important, though. You people are too perfect. Too good. Too wholesome. You're too much alike. You're just not like people really are, Marsha."

"What do you mean?"

"You're like typical TV families. Real people aren't like that. They have arguments. They belch. They fart."

"Fart?"

"Yeah, it's a word you wouldn't know because they don't use it on TV. I guess you thought you'd blend in best if you imitated what you thought were typical families, but we're not completely like TV characters. Hasn't anyone but me noticed, Marsha?"

She sniffled, managed a weak smile, and said: "You are one of the first to get to know one of us. I guess I failed."

As I looked at Marsha, I felt myself drawn to her despite what I knew about her, and that feeling made me angry. "Another thing, Marsha. I don't like being part of your experiment, with you acting like you really liked me."

"It wasn't just an experiment. I *do* like you, Shelley, you *know* that," she said. "I'm not putting on an act about that, Shelley."

I knew I had to be the superchump of all time, because I couldn't help believing her. I nodded and said, "There are more important things at stake, anyway. What are your plans here? Are you"—I felt stupid asking it—"planning to take over our planet?"

She shook her head. "Just blend in, like you said."

"Why?"

"Our world has been getting too crowded, Shelley. For years we've been sending explorers to find other worlds where we can live. When we find a place with people, we study them to see if we can fit in. In some places they shoot our ships down. We can't settle with nasty people like that."

"And here?"

"We've been sending ships for about thirty years—ever since we began picking up your radio and TV signals. Your attitude has been perfect."

"What attitude?"

"You don't believe in us. We can send six flying saucers—as you call them—right over a town, and people will say it was an illusion. Many times we've landed our ships right in the middle of roads. We've even taken people aboard our ships to study them, but nobody ever believes them. We know because we listen in on your radio and TV reports.

"Last year we decided that Earth was ready for settlement. We thought a good way to blend in was as a religious community. We knew from listening to your TV and radio shows at home that you value wholesome, pleasant families, so that's what we modelled ourselves after. It was easy for us. We're a lot like that anyway."

"You mean you're really like the dummies on TV?" I asked.

"Dummies?" she asked, looking offended.

You don't want to offend an alien, so I changed the subject. "My Uncle Myron and I saw a flying saucer go right over our heads last August. Was that you?"

"One of our scout ships probably. In the past couple years we've sent a few ships to test out the area and see how the people would react. It turned out that this area was real good. It's remote. And we didn't hear one report on TV or radio about us. We settlers arrived in three ships just a few weeks ago, and we've got more ships on the way."

"Aren't you afraid now that I know all this?"

She had regained her composure and her friendly smile. "If you tell people we're from a planet eight light years away, they'll think you're crazy, or persecuting us, or something like—"

"*Eight* light years away! It must take you a long time to get here."

"No, our ships can go much faster than light travels. What I was saying, Shelley, is that if you tell people we're from a planet eight light years away, you'll have problems— not us. But why *should* you tell anyone about us, Shelley?" she continued, the soft, cooing tone coming back into her voice. "We don't mean you any harm. All we want is to live in peace with you. We like you folks—and we really enjoy your television."

"You mean as a way to study us?"

"No, we *love* it, Shelley," she sighed. "There's one more thing I should tell you about us, Shelley. We don't value intelligence at all. You see, long ago we almost wiped ourselves out with bombs and stuff. That happened a few times. We finally decided that smartness and creativeness and inventions had caused us to develop technologies that almost destroyed us. Anyway, we don't value those three things anymore. We value enjoying ourselves and acting pleasant. We've had machines do things for us for so long that we don't even know how they work anymore. We don't know much of *anything*, Shelley, but, to us, that's good. At home, smart people are treated as outcasts or even put in jail. Among my people, I'm considered a little too smart. We'd love to settle down here and marry with you and raise nice, pleasant families like on TV. In a few generations, almost everyone on Earth could be like us. Does that sound bad?"

"It doesn't sound right. What about all the books we've written, the beautiful paintings, the philosophy—what about new ideas and achieving things?"

Marsha stared at me with a thoughtful expression, as if thinking about what I had said. "Maybe *you* care about those things, Shelley, but we don't think very many of your people care about them. Reverend Smith says your people are almost like us already. Anyway, you'd like to be. Isn't that why so many of you watch those shows?"

I didn't have any answer for that, but something else bothered me. "What do you really look like, Marsha?" I asked.

"In my real form?" After I nodded, she stared up at a single tiny white cloud that was floating across the sky. She seemed to suddenly make up her mind, and then she said: "I'll show you, Shelley—if you're sure you want to see it." I nodded again and she said, "Okay, Shelley, ready?"

She closed her eyes in concentration. Afraid that she'd turn into some horror, I closed mine, too. When I opened them, I saw a tall, thin, grasshopper-green creature with a small, smiling head, two huge bulging eyes, and very thin arms and legs. She reminded me a little of some friendly lizards I'd seen when our family went to Florida.

Have you ever seen one of those science-fiction movies in which a person gradually turns into a werewolf? She changed back to Marsha in the same slow way. Her head grew in size, her whole body broadened and got shorter, her claws turned into hands, and the blonde hair reappeared on her head.

Once she was Marsha again, she looked at her designer jeans and said, "Oh, gosh, I ripped them doing that. They would have cost fifty dollars in a store." She held out her hand to me and added, in her soft, cooing voice: "I'd still like to be your girl friend, Shelley. I *really* like you."

"No," I said, pulling my hand away.

"I *knew* I shouldn't have let you see what I look like!" she said, with fresh tears in her eyes.

"It wasn't that," I said. "I don't think it's good to count mindlessness so highly."

At that, Marsha burst into a torrent of tears and sank down onto the blanket. Part of me wanted to tell her that I really liked her and wanted to continue our relationship as it had been going. But I knew I couldn't let these mindless aliens blend in with us.

After a couple minutes, she stood up, forced a smile, and said: "Well—*friends* then," and held out her hand for me to shake.

I wouldn't do that either. "If you wanted to live with us you should have asked us, and not pretended to be something you're not, Marsha."

"Shelley, your people would lock us up and do experiments on us if we told them who we are. I hope you won't tell anyone about us, Shelley. *I'm* not going to tell anyone that you know about us, and I like you too much to let anyone hurt you. But I may not be able to help you if my people think you're a threat to them."

That last part scared me. I wanted to be sure Marsha wouldn't think that I was going to try to expose them, so I told her: "You don't have to worry about me telling anyone. If I couldn't convince people about the UFO I saw last summer, I'll never be able to convince anyone about what you people really are."

When we walked our bikes out of the meadow, I noticed a tall pile of junk in the far corner, perhaps a hundred yards away. A sign next to the junk said COPPER CREEK GAR-BAGE DUMP. As I rode home from the garbage dump that I'd thought was a meadow, I was already trying to think of ways to get the aliens off our planet.

10

My Girl Friend, Trish

When I got back to the resort, I found Uncle Myron sitting outside with his shirt off, reading a book called *The Origins of the Universe*. "Uncle Myron, there's something I want to tell you that I don't want my folks to know. Could we go in your office?"

We went inside and sat down on the old torn chairs. "What happened?" he said. "You look shaken up."

I took a deep breath. "You know the flying saucer we saw last summer? The creatures on it are living in Copper Creek."

Uncle Myron's blue eyes looked at me closely. "How do you know that?"

I told him I'd spied on Marsha and her family, and about what had occurred in the "meadow" that morning. When I finished, he said, "Shelley, as much as I respect you, I don't think I'd believe you if I hadn't seen the flying saucer with you last summer. But I've had my own suspicions, and you're not the kind of person who would make all of this up." He rubbed the silver stubble on his face and added,

"Can you picture trying to convince anyone else of this?"
I nodded. "We need some concrete proof," I said.

"Yeah, just one tool or piece of metal that couldn't have come from Earth would do the trick," said Uncle Myron. "I think I'll go into town and observe those folks with what you said in mind, and at the same time I'll try to figure out how we can snoop around there sometime without being seen. I get my allergy pills at the grocery there every month or so, but I'm going to spend even more time there now. I'll wait maybe a week to go, so they don't suspect you told me about them."

"There's some research you could do, Uncle Myron," I told him.

"What?"

"Go into Cottage One and watch TV a lot. Then when you go to town, you'll see just how much they're like TV characters."

My picnic with Marsha and that talk with Uncle Myron occurred on Tuesday, June 25, 1985. I've got all the details of what happened written in red ink in my diary.

The next morning Jane, Cynthia, and I went over to Cottage One at about nine, the same as usual. "Leave It to Beaver" was about halfway over when Uncle Myron knocked on the door. After a couple hours, I sat next to him on the couch and pointed things out to him while Jane and Cynthia played Barbies on the floor.

When an ad came on, I told Uncle Myron, "See that guy squeezing the toilet paper? Doesn't he look a lot like the grocer, Mr. Davis?"

99

Uncle Myron stared at the man and said, "Maybe. I don't know. Yeah, I see it—*definitely.*"

Jane looked up from dressing her Ken doll and asked, "Who looks like the man on TV?"

"Nobody, Morrie, forget it," I said.

After that I turned the TV up louder and spoke quietly to Uncle Myron. We watched TV the rest of the morning. When it was time for the newsbreak, Uncle Myron invited us over to his room for lunch. He made peanut butter and jelly sandwiches for us and gave us bottles of pop. After lunch we went back and watched some more TV. During "The Brady Bunch," I was staring at the youngest sister and feeling real sad when Jane looked up from the painting she was making and asked me, "What's the matter, Shelley?"

So hypnotized was I by the image of the girl who looked like Marsha that I hadn't realized there were tears in my eyes. I wiped them away and said, "Nothing, Morrie."

I didn't feel like watching "The Brady Bunch," so I left Uncle Myron doing his TV research and went into my room to take a short nap. Somehow I woke up about an hour later thinking of Trish Vincent. I went to Cottage Ten and got permission from Mom and Dad to ride my bike to Odell.

About forty minutes later, I approached the pretty little town of Odell nestled in the hills. First I stopped at a gas station to fill the Schwinn's tires with air, then I rode up the hill on Iron Street and leaned the bike against the wall of the diner. I walked into the diner and sat down in my torn-leather booth.

Trish was behind the counter talking to an old man who was drinking a cup of coffee on the end stool. I was starting to think that Trish was going to ignore me when she went to the fountain, mixed a cherry Coke, and brought it to me.

"How'd you know that's what I wanted?" I asked.

"I just took a wild guess," she said, with a little smile.

Before she walked away, I asked: "Did you have a nice year, Trish?"

"Better than I thought. School wasn't bad, and I've got a couple friends. Anyway, we're moving back to Detroit at the end of the summer. My dad got a job there."

She walked away and began cleaning the counter with a cloth. I was noticing that Trish's red bangs were cut beautifully uneven across her forehead when her aunt came out of the kitchen with a plate of roast beef, mashed potatoes, and gravy for the old man. I picked up my cherry Coke and went to sit near the spot Trish was wiping off.

I couldn't think of what to say to her. "That girl I was with Monday night?" I finally said. "She's just a friend I made when I went into Copper Creek one time."

"That's nice," Trish said, continuing to wipe the counter.

"I mean, she's not my girl friend or anything."

She looked at me disgustedly and said, "You can go to the movies with anyone you want, anytime you want."

Boy, did that bring me back to earth. Now *that's* the way real people talk to me. It made Marsha seem all the more unreal.

"You know," I said. "I always say the wrong thing to you.

101

I'm really a shy—look at this," I said in frustration. I pulled out my wallet and began to unfold a cartoon. "Let me sh—"

I wanted to show her a cartoon I'd made of her over the winter. In this particular drawing, the lever of the Coke machine had gotten stuck and there was a Coke flood on the floor. Trish was standing on a chair saying, in a blurb next to her mouth: DOES ANYBODY WANT AN EXTRA-LARGE COKE? The problem was that as I unfolded the drawing, my hand slipped and knocked the cherry Coke over. The liquid floated across the counter and struck the hand of the old man, who looked down at the reddish black bubbles and then over at me.

"I'm sorry, I'm such a klutz. Here, look at this," I said, handing her my cartoon. While Trish studied it, I took her cloth and wiped off the counter, all the way down to the old man.

"Are you going to be a cartoonist?" Trish asked.

"If I can. What about you?"

"I'd like to be an Olympic speed skater and then maybe a veterinarian. Anything but a waitress would be good."

"Do you have to practice a lot to be a speed skater?"

"In the winter I practice two hours a day after school at the outdoor skating rink near the high school. At home in Detroit we have an indoor rink, and I practice at least an hour almost every day of the year."

"You call Detroit home even though you've lived here for more than a year?"

"I think of it as home. We're moving back there in the fall—as soon as Dad's done working for Harv."

102

"Harv Holmquist?" I asked.

"Yeah, my dad works as a logger for him. Just a second, Shelley." Trish disappeared into the kitchen and returned a few minutes later with a newspaper clipping, which she handed to me. It told how she'd come in first in a speed-skating contest in Detroit.

"The only time I ever skated, I spent most of the time with my butt on the ice," I told Trish. "Except for playing fast-pitch with George Parkinson and intramural softball, I'm not really very athletic."

Trish asked me what fast-pitch was, and I explained that it was like baseball. "First you need a wall," I said. "You draw a box on the wall for a strike zone. Then you make boundaries for singles, doubles, triples, and home runs."

"When can we play it?" Trish asked.

"How about after work today?"

"I don't get off for two hours."

"I'll be back!" I excitedly told her.

I rode my bike over to the library to use the outdoor phone. I called the resort and asked Uncle Myron to ask Mom if it was okay for me to stay out late. When he returned to the phone, he told me it was fine so long as I got home before it was dark. I passed the time until 5:00 eating a few eclairs at the bakery and buying a couple balls, a cheap bat, and a light for the Schwinn at the Odell Bike and Sports Shop.

At 5:00 I rode my bike back to the Odell Diner, then I waited outside until ten minutes past, when Trish came out. "Sorry I'm late, the evening waitress just got here," she said. She asked me to wait there for five minutes. When she came downstairs her red hair was back in a ponytail and she was wearing a blue sweatshirt.

Trish told me that the Odell Elementary School, a couple blocks away, had a good wall where we could play. I pulled the bat and balls out of the slats of the Schwinn's basket, left the bike in front of the diner, and walked with Trish to the school.

There were already a number of batter's boxes painted onto the wall. We picked a box, made boundaries, and started the game.

I'm not one of those guys who can't take losing to a girl, and I'm not an excuse maker, either, but there were a couple reasons why I had trouble against Trish. See, I was figuring that she was a girl and didn't know the game, so that I could take it easy on her at first and then try harder later. The problem was that Trish was a really good athlete, and once she got used to the game she was really good at it. She could pitch fast and accurately, and she kept lining hits into the sandbox and past the swings. When I realized that I was losing to a female at my best sport, I started to panic a little, and that made me play worse. By the time I finally lined a home run into the cemetery for my first run, I was down 7–1.

As Trish and I searched among the tombstones for the ball, she said, "Nice hit, Shelley."

"About time," I said. "I had no idea you were *this* good an athlete."

"I'm having fun," she said. As we climbed back onto the playground, Trish added, "Don't you wish you could play the first inning over?" and gave me a playful poke in the ribs.

With defeat staring me in the face like that, I put the fact that Trish was a girl out of my mind, and that helped. I made a little comeback near the end, and only lost 12–6.

We were discussing the game on our way back to the diner when we passed the Odell Theatre. Marsha and her parents were waiting in a short line near the front of the theater. Marsha turned red when we passed and glared at Trish, but Mr. and Mrs. Coe and I said "Hi" to each other. I noticed that Mr. Coe now had little wrinkles around his eyes and slight touches of gray in his hair. He no longer looked so much like Mr. Brady, but you probably wouldn't notice the change unless you'd studied him closely, as I had. As for Mrs. Coe, she no longer had her beehive hairstyle, so she didn't look quite so much like the "Happy Days" mom.

When we neared the diner, I was tempted to tell Trish about Marsha and her people. It would have been really nice to tell someone besides Uncle Myron, but I refrained from doing it. Can you imagine how she would have reacted if I had told her that the beautiful girl we'd just passed was really a six-foot-tall lizard?

The rest of that evening was great. Trish asked me upstairs, where I got to meet her Aunt Theresa, the lady who owned the Odell Diner, and her father, a small man with a little black moustache and the strongest-looking arm muscles I'd ever seen beneath his cutoff Montreal Canadiens sweatshirt. Trish's aunt invited me for dinner, and when I called up my mom to ask her, she said it was fine.

Trish and I made a salad and Aunt Theresa made a great beef stew, and we had a fine time together. During dessert (cookies that Trish had made), Mr. Vincent told me that he had been born in Canada, and somehow we then got on the subject of school. "My Trishie is weak in math," he told me, staring at me with his huge black eyes. When I said that I was pretty good at math, Mr. Vincent asked, "Well, then, could you give her a few math pointers this summer?"

"I'd love to," I answered. A little while later we tossed the Schwinn into the back of Mr. Vincent's pickup, and he and Trish gave me a ride home and even came in to meet my parents. I went to sleep that night thinking how great it was to be with real people—especially Trish—and to get my mind off the aliens.

During the next three or four days, Trish and I played another fast-pitch game (which I won) and went bowling in Odell and blew quite a few quarters on video games at the McElhenny Dime Store. One thing I noticed during those days was that the Copper Creekers were starting to spend a lot of time in Odell. One day Trish and I were inside the Odell Bank changing our dollars into quarters, and the person ahead of us turned around after conducting his business—and it was Mr. Coe. Another time Trish and I were eating pasties (meat-filled pastries that are very popular in Upper Michigan) at the bakery, and I heard a familiar voice telling a joke—and there was Nils Cregar buying a birthday cake.

On Saturday night, Mom invited Trish and her dad and

Aunt Theresa over for a barbecue. Trish's aunt brought along her special sauce, and we had the tastiest spareribs you ever ate, along with Dad's famous Caesar salad. Afterwards, Uncle Myron took out his telescope and showed everyone the planets and stars. At about ten in the evening, Mr. Vincent yawned and said, "Ready to hit the trail, Trishie?"

"I'll drive her home if she wants to look through the telescope longer," Dad offered. Mr. Vincent said that was fine with him. As he and Aunt Theresa drove off in the pickup, Dad, Mom, and Uncle Myron headed inside. "Let us know when Trish is ready to go," Dad called to us. "Come on, Jane and Cynthia."

"We want to stay out with Shelley and Trish," Jane said.

"Inside!" Mom said to Jane and Cynthia. "Shelley and Trish are old enough to stay up later, but it's time for hot chocolate and then bed for you two."

When Trish and I were alone, I aimed the telescope at the large orange moon rising above the treetops. I showed her the mountains and craters and the flat areas they called *maria* while she "oohed" and "aahed." As she looked through the telescope, I noticed how the moon brought out all the lovely red hues in her hair and how there was an awestruck, intelligent look in her eyes.

After the moon, I aimed Uncle Myron's telescope at the Milky Way and told her to look in the eyepiece while sweeping the telescope across the sky. "I never knew there were so many stars," she said. When she looked up from the telescope, I reached over and took her hand. Trish came close to me and gave me a sweet, wonderful kiss on the mouth that lasted for about a second. Then she pointed to a star and said, "Show me that one, Shelley." She was my girl friend from that moment on.

11

A Close Call

A couple days after Trish and her dad and aunt came over for the barbecue, Uncle Myron decided to go into Copper Creek. As Jane, Cynthia, and I watched TV in Cottage One, I kept looking out the window for Uncle Myron's blue convertible to return. At about 11:30 I heard the crunch of wheels on the gravel driveway, and I ran outside to meet him. Right away I saw that he looked a little pale and upset. I followed him inside the office and into his bedroom, where he lay down on his bed alongside Randa.

"I noticed what you said about them being like TV characters," said Uncle Myron, tossing Randa a loose Chee-to that he found beneath a blanket. "They're made of bits and pieces of different characters—the voice of one, the gestures of another, the personality of another. I wouldn't have noticed it if you hadn't pointed it out to me, but with that in mind I saw it.

"I went into the appliance store and told them I was looking around for a new TV. When I told Mr. Coe my name, he asked me if I was your uncle, and then he asked if I knew why you and Marsha weren't friends anymore. I told him I had no idea, but that I'd heard she was a very nice girl. I don't think he suspected that you told me about them.

"After I left the TV store, I went to get some things at Mr. Davis's store, and I saw the resemblance to the man in the toilet-paper ad. Since they're supposed to be a religious community, I then went to that huge church of theirs, knocked on the minister's office, and told him I wanted to meet him. He's a big guy with a southern accent named Smith, friendly as can be. While I was talking to him, I heard a hum, but I couldn't tell from where. After saying good-bye I pretended to leave the church, but as soon as Reverend Smith went back in his office I sneaked back inside. I looked in several rooms but still couldn't tell where the hum was coming from. Then I went downstairs into the basement. As soon as I got down there, I could tell that the hum was coming from behind a door. I tried it, but it was locked. As I was standing there, though, a man opened the door. I saw the strangest things inside."

"What?"

"It looked like a huge warehouse with all kinds of things like couches and bookcases. On one side of the warehouse were some weird machines that looked like metal boxes. Two men were putting junk—metal and plastic and so on—into them. I only saw inside for a second, and then the guy who opened the door spotted me standing there. All I could think to say was that I had just visited with Reverend Smith and was looking for the toilet. He pointed upstairs, and I left. I was really frightened when he caught me there—

110

more frightened than I can ever remember—maybe because they seem so nice and we don't really know how dangerous they are."

"What do you think we should do now?" I asked him.

"In a few days, I'm going to go to Mr. Davis's store, pick up my allergy medicine the same as always, and act as natural as I can. I don't want them to suspect that you've told me anything about them. While I'm there, I'm going to try to find out if there's a time when I can get in the church when no one's around, so I can get a closer look at those machines. They might be the concrete proof we're looking for."

"I'll go with you if we get a chance to see the machines."

"No!" he said. "Shelley, maybe they think *I'm* on to them and maybe they don't, but Marsha knows *you're* on to them. Marsha even told you that if they feel you're a threat, some of them could hurt you. How would it be if they found you sneaking around Copper Creek?"

"But, Uncle Myron," I said, "when they saw you down in the basement, they must have realized that you know about them. It'll be just as dangerous for you to try to spy on them. Let's go together."

"*No!*" he repeated, sounding annoyed this time. "Let me put it another way. How many people know the truth about the Copper Creekers?"

"Just you and me."

"We can't *both* risk getting caught spying on them. If something happens to both of us, who'll be left to do anything about them?"

When Uncle Myron saw that I agreed with that, he said, "I think I need to take a nap now, I'm pretty tired. Oh, and Shelley," he added, just as I was leaving, "don't tell Trish about any of this. We don't want to get her involved. And something else. I don't want you riding your bike into Odell to meet Trish anymore. I don't think it's good for you to ride past downtown Copper Creek on that lonely road. Whenever you want to go to Odell, just tell me and I'll be glad to give you a lift. There're lots of books I want to read. I might as well do it at the library, and I might as well give you a lift into town when I go there."

Uncle Myron had to drive me to Odell quite a bit, because I was spending nearly every afternoon and evening with Trish. I'd meet her after work and we'd go to a movie or play fast-pitch or just hang out around town while Uncle Myron read at the library. When the library closed at 9:00, I'd meet my uncle there and we'd drive home together.

On the day that Uncle Myron was going into Copper Creek to get his allergy tablets (Friday, July 5, according to my diary), Trish and I planned to see *Cinderella* at the Odell Theatre. Uncle Myron dropped me off in front of the diner at 4:30 and told me that he'd meet me at the library at 9:00 to take me home.

I went into the diner and had two free hamburgers while I waited for Trish to get off work. When she got off and had her dinner, I had another hamburger to keep her company. At a few minutes after five, we were walking down the street toward the theater when we heard the roar of a car engine. There was a sudden squeal of brakes and then a crash.

When we got to the theater, we saw a very upset-looking woman sitting behind the wheel of the car that had been struck. Behind the wheel of the souped-up old red car that had hit her was Marsha's brother, Dwayne.

As Dwayne slammed his car door, I was startled to see the change in him. He was wearing a black leather jacket with DWAYNE embroidered over the pocket, and he had a tough look on his face. "Lady, you stopped too fast," he said.

"I was going slow, and you slammed into *me!*" said the woman, who was so upset that she could barely talk.

Dwayne made a face and said, "*Slow* is right—you were driving like a turtle." His face still looked a lot like the Fonz's, but there was something really mean about his expression. As I stared at him, it came to me. A couple weeks earlier, Jane and Cynthia and I had watched a trashy movie called *Motorcycle Maniac* on TV. Dwayne was acting like the kid who had played the Motorcycle Maniac.

"There oughta be a law against people driving—" Dwayne began, but he was interrupted by the blare of Chief McMaster's siren.

We onlookers tightened our circle so that we could hear Chief McMaster talk to Dwayne, the woman, and the witnesses. After he was done, the chief said, "This is your second ticket, Dwayne. I don't know what your dad's gonna think when he finds out about this. All right folks, get going." The woman was able to drive her car away, and a minute later the only signs that there had been an accident were some pieces of broken red plastic from her taillight.

Because of the accident, Trish and I had missed the

beginning of *Cinderella*, so we decided to see it another night and go watch softball. We walked over to Riggs Field, which was carved out of the woods next to Riggs Tavern.

While the players took batting practice, I noticed a black leather jacket on one of the team benches. I glanced around the field and spotted Dwayne shagging flies near the home-run fence. I could hear him talking about his accident with his teammates, saying things like "What an old hag!" I wondered why Dwayne had changed his personality.

I was still thinking about Dwayne when something else caught my attention. I looked across the bleachers, and there, just a few yards away, were Marsha and her parents sitting in the top row. Usually when you look at a person who is staring at you, the person quickly looks away, but Marsha just kept looking back and forth from Trish to me. I could tell that she was jealous that I was with Trish, and that worried me.

"Why don't we go get ice-cream cones instead of watching this game?" I asked Trish. But she said that she wanted to see the game because it might help her come up with a new strategy for beating me at fast-pitch.

Once the game started, Dwayne swore and argued with the umpire more than anyone on the field, but his teammates didn't mind because he hit three titanic home runs. "Way to go, Dwayne!" they said each time, slapping him on the back. Dwayne caught for his team, and on one close play when the ump called the runner safe at home plate, Dwayne got furious. He kicked dirt at the ump and said: "He missed home dish by a mile!"

"I'm going to throw you out of this game in a second, son!" the umpire warned. "And it's called home *plate*."

"Oh, yeah," Dwayne said, looking up at his family in the bleachers.

"Now, Dwayne, take it easy," Mr. Coe called down to him. "I don't know what I can do about that boy's temper," Mr. Coe added loudly.

Several spectators around the Coes said, "I know what you mean," and "My boy's the same way," and "He'll outgrow it."

As the game resumed, I heard Mrs. Coe say, "Those baseball pants'll be a real challenge for my new bleach." She then got into a discussion about bleaches with some ladies near her. Then and throughout the game, I felt Marsha staring down at us.

When the game ended Trish and I walked back to the diner. After she unlocked the door with her key, we went inside and each had a Dreamsicle and an ice-cream bar. We were just finishing the tasty little last part stuck to the ice-cream bar sticks when I saw that it was almost 9:00. Sitting there in our booth, Trish gave me a little kiss as we'd been doing lately, and then we went outside and she locked up.

"I'll walk you to your uncle," Trish said, and then accompanied me up the street, which was so deserted that I could hear the chirps of the crickets echoing off the walls of the buildings.

My uncle's empty convertible was parked outside the library. Trish and I leaned against the car and talked for a while until Uncle Myron came out of the library. Trish

115

waved at him and said, "Hi, Mr. Silver," and then added, "'Bye, Shelley," and started to walk home.

Trish had turned the corner and Uncle Myron and I were just pulling out when suddenly I heard an engine roar and then a loud squeal of tires. Uncle Myron did a 180-degree turn, gunned it around the corner, and pulled up next to Trish, who was standing by the curb about a hundred feet from the diner and looking real scared.

"That crazy Dwayne nearly ran me down!" said Trish, who was so upset she could barely talk. "The guy who slammed into the woman's car today. If I hadn't dived away, he might have killed me." She stared at Uncle Myron and me as if hoping we could offer some explanation.

"You make it sound like he did it on purpose," said Uncle Myron, glancing at me.

Trish nodded. "He saw me and pulled away, and for a second I thought he was kidding, but he didn't stop. Why would he want to run me down?"

"Take it easy, Trish, you're all right," Uncle Myron kept telling her, as we walked Trish up the stairs to her apartment.

When Mr. Vincent heard about what had happened, he became so upset that he couldn't dial, so he had me phone Chief McMaster. Mr. Vincent became even more upset as he and Trish spoke to the chief. "I know it was on purpose because Trish *said* it was on purpose!" Mr. Vincent yelled into the phone. Then he said, "Just a second," and covered the phone. "Did anyone see what happened?" he asked Trish, who shook her head no.

"He says he can't give him more than a ticket for *almost* hitting a pedestrian," Mr. Vincent told us, after the conversation was finished. "He says Dwayne's wild but that he doesn't think he would do something like this on purpose. He's going over to talk to Dwayne now. Well," added Mr. Vincent bitterly, "*I* can give him something more than a ticket."

Uncle Myron had a tough time convincing Mr. Vincent that he shouldn't go after Dwayne with his deer rifle. Finally Uncle Myron said, "If that cop doesn't do anything about it, then maybe you should do something—but I don't know how it's going to be for Trish to have her one living parent locked in jail for killing someone." That calmed him down and got him to agree to wait to see what happened.

On the way home, Uncle Myron and I had a lot to talk about. "Why do you think Dwayne's gone so crazy?" I asked my uncle.

"It sounds like they've decided they'll seem more like real people if they're not all so goody-goody, but when they turn bad they turn really bad, just like the bad guys on TV."

"Do you think Marsha had Dwayne try to run down Trish because she was jealous?" I asked my uncle, when we neared the lights of downtown Copper Creek.

"It could be, or it could be that Dwayne just decided he'd help his sister by getting rid of her rival. I think that's more likely than that Marsha would ask him to do it. But what's the difference? The thing is, will he try it again? What can we do? We can't tell Trish's father the truth about the situation yet, can we? I think the best thing is for you and Trish to stay close to the diner and her apartment when you're in town, and for

117

us to do something about the aliens as soon as possible.

"There's one good piece of news that may help us do that, Shelley. When I went to Copper Creek today to get my allergy pills, I learned that the Copper Creekers are having a town picnic a week from this Sunday. Mr. Davis told me everyone in town's going, and the people from Odell are also invited. With everyone out at the picnic, I think I'll be able to get into the church basement and find what we need to prove that the Copper Creekers aren't from our planet."

12

"Such Pleasant Folks"

The next morning, I awoke to the sound of a telephone ringing in the distance. Before another fifteen seconds had passed, I had my pants on over my pajamas and was rushing into Uncle Myron's office. My uncle talked for a while to Mr. Vincent, who I could tell had calmed down a little, and then Trish came on and told me that Chief McMaster had just phoned. The upshot was that Dwayne had insisted he hadn't seen Trish when he'd sped out of the parking space. He was probably going to lose his license because of all his tickets, but first he had to be convicted of the offenses at his trials.

"What's your father think of this?" I asked Trish.

"He's still mad, but he keeps asking if I'm sure it was on purpose. The more I think about it, the more I wonder if maybe Dwayne just didn't see me. I just can't think of any reason why he would want to run me down."

It's not pleasant to believe that someone really tried to kill you, so Trish was kidding herself, just like I'd kidded myself about them not being aliens. "I guess it could have been an accident," I said, and then made a date to see her later in the afternoon.

After I hung up the phone, I asked my uncle why we couldn't tell Trish about the aliens now.

"If we tell Trish and then her father finds out about it and starts making noise, we may be putting his life in danger, too. It's July sixth today, Shelley. The picnic is the fourteenth. Let's try to make it until the picnic without any disasters, and if we can find the proof we need, we can tell the whole *world* about it then. Meanwhile, we need a plan for breaking into the church. I'll go into Copper Creek this week and try to figure out the best way to get in there."

During the next few days, I made it a point to be with Trish much of the time—all the while watching for speeding cars and other dangers. Uncle Myron would drop me off at the diner at about ten in the morning, and I'd hang out there reading and drawing cartoons. When there weren't any customers at the diner and after the diner closed, I'd give Trish some math pointers.

On the night of Tuesday, July 9, Uncle Myron and I were riding home from Odell in his car when he told me he'd come up with a plan. "After I dropped you off this morning, I took a spin into Copper Creek," he explained. "I bought some things at the Davis Grocery and then I walked by the church. There's a bunch of windows on the outside, and I don't think it'll be very hard to get in. What I need to do is break into the church very early that Sunday morning, before anyone's awake, wait there, and then when the commotion of the picnic begins, go down into the basement."

"But you said the room with the weird machines is locked," I said.

"I'll try to get into the locked room some way. Even if I don't, I'm sure there'll be times that the church is empty and I'll be able to look for the proof we need in Reverend Smith's office and other rooms. I'm going to pack myself a few sandwiches before I go in there, because I may have to hide out in the church a couple days. There's a room down in the basement filled with folding chairs, and I think I could hide out there without being noticed. Who knows, maybe I'll get a picture of one of them turning into a lizard. Oh, Shelley, open that bag in the backseat."

I reached back and pulled the bag onto my lap. Inside were a beautiful new 35-millimeter camera and some high-speed film for shooting indoors without a flash.

"What if they catch you?" I asked.

"We'll figure out how much time we'll give me to spend in there. If I'm not back home by a certain time, you'll tell your parents and Chief McMaster. It's not a perfect plan, I know, but it's the best I've come up with."

"I wish I could go with you," I said.

"Shelley, if something happens to me while doing this, you're going to have to figure out a way to get the proof yourself. We need solid proof to convince people that the Copper Creekers are aliens so we can force them to leave."

That night while I was in bed waiting to fall asleep, I thought of something that would help our plan along. The next morning, Wednesday, July 10, I hurried over to the office to tell Uncle Myron my idea.

"Uncle Myron!" I called from the office. There was no answer. I knew I'd seen his car parked on the gravel driveway, but I looked out the window to make sure. "Uncle Myron!" I called again. This time Randa came out of Uncle Myron's room, wagging her tail in a puzzled way. I followed her into Uncle Myron's room, but in the darkness all I could see was his curled-up shape in bed. "Uncle Myron?" I said, just a bit louder than a whisper. I put my hand gently on his shoulder and shook it, but still he didn't respond.

I turned on the light and was glad to find that at least his eyes were open, but they didn't seem to be seeing me. Randa was whimpering now and sniffing at his hand, which was hanging over the side of the bed. I picked up his hand and squeezed it, thinking maybe he'd had some kind of a stroke but was still alive. His hand felt cool and limp, and when I let go it swung like a pendulum.

I was whimpering now, just like Randa, as I walked back and forth around the bed to look at Uncle Myron from different angles. "Uncle Myron! Uncle Myron!" I kept saying, hoping that at any second he would blink and show me that he was at least alive. I shook his shoulder, rubbed the scar on his right cheek, and even shouted his name into his ear. I was standing there looking at his eyes when it finally sank in that Uncle Myron was dead. At that moment I ran out of the room to Mom and Dad.

They came over right away, took a look at him, and called the hospital. An ambulance came and took Uncle Myron away. Jane and Cynthia had awakened, and I had to watch over them while Mom and Dad drove away after the ambulance. Jane began to bawl and say, "Maybe he's still alive," and that made me cry like a baby. About a half hour later, Mom and Dad came back and told me that my uncle had died of a heart attack. I knew Uncle Myron had had an attack years ago, so at first I didn't question the hospital's explanation for his death.

It's a Jewish custom to hold a funeral soon after someone dies, so Uncle Myron's was planned for the next day. There weren't any Jewish funeral places in the area, so it was held at the Olson-McDeavett Funeral Home. We went, and Harv and Betty Holmquist came, and so did Trish and her dad and Aunt Theresa. Grandma Anna—my mom's mother and Uncle Myron's older sister—wanted to take a Greyhound bus up there, but she'd broken her hip over the winter, so Mom convinced her to stay home.

We buried Uncle Myron next to the Olsons and Swensons in the cemetery right next to where Trish and I had played fast-pitch. After we had taken turns putting the first shovelfuls of dirt over him, Mom said, "I just can't believe it."

"I can't either," said Harv, wiping away his tears with the back of his big hand. "I know Mike had a heart attack about ten years ago, but he was so *alive*."

Right then it came to me, standing there in the Odell Cemetery. *They* had killed him. I didn't know how they had done it, but I knew why. When they'd seen him snooping around the basement they'd realized that he knew about them. Probably they knew about me, too, and the only thing that had kept them from killing me was that they figured a kid couldn't do much about them. With those thoughts, everything suddenly turned dark, and I felt dizzy and weak. As we left the cemetery, I had to hold on to Dad.

As soon as we got home, Mom took Jane and Cynthia into the living room to give them a talk about death. But after changing my clothes, I went to Uncle Myron's room and locked the door behind me. There was an old chest of drawers next to his bed, and I looked through it for a clue. Most of the drawers had socks, underwear, and pajamas stuffed into them, and just looking at those things that Uncle Myron had worn made me cry again.

A drawer in the middle had papers and other important-looking things in it, so I carefully pulled the whole thing out and placed it on the bed. In the left-hand corner of the drawer was a blue box, but the old legal papers inside were of no help. I also found some books in the drawer on astronomy and birds, and an old photo album that contained pictures of Uncle Myron with his wife when they were young. In addition, I found a few pictures that Jane had drawn for Uncle Myron, about half a dozen friendship rings and pins, a letter I'd sent him, and two wristwatches. I put the drawer back without having found anything out of the ordinary.

I looked through his wastebasket, inside the lamp table next to his bed, under his bed, and among the newspapers, clothes, and pop cans on the floor. I opened his closet and found a bunch of clothes and shoes, his telescope, and a half-done painting of some familiar-looking people. Studying the picture, I realized that they were supposed to be Mom, Dad, Jane, and me.

I sat down in the middle of Uncle Myron's bed with my

legs crossed, and thought. If they'd killed him, they must have come into contact with him in some way. Uncle Myron had recently gone into Copper Creek on several occasions, I remembered. He'd gone to the Davis Grocery several times, and just a few days before he'd picked up something he got at the grocery every month or so. It was some kind of medicine—his allergy pills!

The allergy pills were lying right on the little lamp table next to his bed. I hadn't paid any attention to them because they were a name brand you can get anywhere. As I held the pills close to my face and stared at them, my hands started shaking and I broke out into a cold sweat. The next second I felt a very cold anger surge through me like a tidal wave. My girl friend had been nearly run down and my uncle probably had been poisoned by the aliens. Sitting there on the edge of Uncle Myron's bed, I vowed that I would stop them if it took my last breath to do it.

I placed the allergy tablets in a paper bag I took from the wastebasket, stuffed the bag into my back pocket, and told my parents I was going to Odell. By the time I reached Grand View Hospital in Odell about a half hour later, my legs were so exhausted from pedalling I could barely walk. I told the receptionist that I needed something analyzed, and she pointed the way to the laboratory.

A nameplate atop the half-door of the laboratory said LLOYD HOPKINS, M.T. "I have something I need analyzed, Mr. Hopkins," I told the balding, very thin man who had his back to me as he poured yellow liquids into test tubes.

"Analyzed for what?" he said, wheeling around.

125

When I saw the thin, smiling face and the little blond moustache, I dropped the pills to the floor. "Nothing," I said, and then picked up the pills and walked away. Mr. Hopkins was one of the Copper Creekers.

I'd done something dumb, I realized, as I rushed out of the hospital. I was the only one left who knew the true nature of the Copper Creekers. If something happened to me, nobody would know. The first thing I should have done after Uncle Myron's death was tell someone else—Trish—about them. I got on my bike, quickly rode over to the diner, and sat down on a stool at the opposite end from the old man who so often ate there.

"Trish, there's something I've got to tell you about," I said, quietly. "Can you get away for a couple minutes?"

"I can't now, Shelley," she answered.

"Trish," I said, "there's something really weird about those people from Copper Creek—come with me for just two minutes."

I'd spoken too loudly, because the old man suddenly asked, "What do you mean—*weird*—son? They're such pleasant folks. Besides, they're reopening the copper mine, and that means jobs for a lot of people in Odell. I thought you young people had open minds about folks who're a little different."

I walked Trish into the entranceway of her apartment and went with her up to the landing. We sat down on the top step just outside her front door, and I told her everything about the Copper Creekers. When I finished, I saw that Trish looked very upset. "Sounds crazy, doesn't it?" I asked.

When Trish just nodded, I asked, "Do you believe it?" and held my breath.

My girl friend nodded again right away and said, "You couldn't have imagined Marsha turning into a monster."

I was so relieved that I gave her a kiss as we sat right there on that top step. "My Uncle Myron came up with a plan that I'm going to follow," I told Trish. "I'll be back right after you get off work to tell it to you."

While waiting for Trish to get off work, I went to the library. When I entered the reference room, I saw a familiar beautiful blonde head bent over a huge art book. I started to walk out of the room, but she said, "Hello, Shelley," in her soft, cooing voice.

I was tempted to confront her about Uncle Myron's death and about her brother's nearly running over Trish, but I knew that it was best for me not to reveal my suspicions. "Hi, Marsha," I said, returning her stare for a second. Then I walked out and went down to the children's room.

I spent the rest of the afternoon in the children's room working on my plan, and then at 5:00 I returned to the diner and told it to Trish. Just as I'd complained about not being able to go with Uncle Myron when he'd planned to break into the church, Trish complained about not being able to go with me.

"*No*, I have to go by myself," I told Trish, and realized that I sounded very much like Uncle Myron when I said it. "If we both get caught, there'll be no one left to do anything about them. You have to stay behind in case something happens to me."

13

Last-Second Preparations

I wanted to be one hundred percent prepared for breaking into the church on Sunday, because my only chance for success was to do everything right. Friday morning I went into the little utility room inside the office and found Uncle Myron's toolbox. I took a wrench, a screwdriver, and several other tools that might help me and placed them in my backpack. Then I loaded Uncle Myron's new camera with film and zipped it up into a separate section.

After that I asked Mom if I could borrow her tape recorder for two or three days and have a couple blank tapes. (Mom sometimes tapes her poems to see how they sound.) The morning I discovered Uncle Myron's body, I had been going to tell him that he should bring a tape recorder along. Mom lent me the recorder and the tapes. After zipping them in, I stuffed the entire backpack behind the office counter.

Somehow, once I had the backpack ready, I realized that I was really going to be breaking into the church on Sunday, and that made me feel real nervous. I was thinking that in two days I'd be risking my life to obtain proof about the aliens when it suddenly occurred to me that there was a huge flaw in my plan. What if I did obtain the proof? I needed someone important to show it to who could do something about the aliens.

I knew I couldn't deal with newspapers and magazines, because that would take too long. That left TV or radio. There was a small TV station in Odell—WKRL. I remembered that Uncle Myron had spoken to an announcer at the station who had been interested in the flying saucer we had seen. I was familiar with the announcer, Ollie Rasmusson, because he was all over the place on that station. Every morning he did a dopey children's show called "Ollie's Place" in which he dressed up as a dragon, in the evening he did the news, and on Saturday he hosted the afternoon "Creature Features" movie. I phoned the station and asked to speak to him, and within a few seconds I was talking to Ollie himself.

"Yel-lo!" he said, sounding like he was in a real hurry. I told him I was the nephew of the man who had seen the flying saucer and that I had seen it, too. I explained that I knew that the station manager wouldn't run a flying saucer story without evidence. Then I asked, "What if I brought you proof that aliens were living right around here?"

For a second I thought he was going to hang up, but then he asked, "How old are you?"

"I'm not just making a crank call!" I said. "I'm offering you the biggest story you're ever going to have in your life. If I get the proof, you'll be the first one I'll bring it to. All you have to do is promise me you'll put it on the air and give me a phone number and address where I can reach you Sunday."

"If you brought proof that aliens were living around here, do you think any broadcaster would pass up the story?" asked Ollie. He sounded as though ninety-nine percent of him still thought it was a crackpot call, but that he didn't want to take a chance and just shrug it off. Although Ollie hadn't actually promised to run the story if I brought proof, I figured that this was the best I could get out of anybody in the news business. He told me he'd be at the station doing the newsbreaks starting at eleven on Sunday, and then said he had to go.

I wanted to see Trish that Friday morning, but I was afraid to ride my bike to Odell because I didn't want to ride past downtown Copper Creek. Fortunately, Cynthia had to go back to Chicago that morning. Mom and Dad were driving into Odell to drop her off at the Greyhound station and to talk to Uncle Myron's lawyer. Jane and I accompanied them. When we entered Odell, I saw that all the store windows had signs in them saying

COME ONE, COME ALL!
1ST ANNUAL COPPER CREEK TOWN PICNIC
EVERYONE FROM ODELL INVITED!
BEER! BRATWURST! RIDES! GAMES!
$3.00 ADULTS, $1.50 KIDS
SUNDAY, JULY 14TH

After we took Cynthia Fender to the bus station, Jane and I went to the diner while Mom and Dad went to talk to Uncle Myron's lawyer. As Jane and I sat eating french fries and drinking cherry Cokes, I picked up an Odell *Daily Globe* that was lying on the table. I still have that Friday, July 12, 1985, newspaper. One of the lead articles told about the Copper Creek picnic. There was another article of note that began

> It has been confirmed that the Copper Creek mine will open August 1. Copper Creek mayor Nils Cregar says that persons interested in obtaining jobs at the mine should contact . . .

On the Marriages and Engagements page was this announcement.

> Reverend and Mrs. Albert Smith III of Copper Creek are pleased to announce the engagement of their daughter, Patricia Suzanne, to Mr. William McMaster of Odell.
>
> The bride-to-be is a secretary at the Copper Creek Universal Humanist Church in Copper Creek. The groom, who is the son of Police Chief Earl G. McMaster and Ida McMaster, is employed in a clerical capacity at McElhenny's Dime Store in Odell.
>
> The wedding, planned for December 22, will be held in the Copper Creek Humanist Church. The bride-to-be's father, the Reverend Albert Smith III, will officiate.
>
> The couple has not yet decided where they will reside.

There were also small articles in the paper saying that Rob Coe was running for the school board and that a group of citizens wanted Nils Cregar, the Copper Creek mayor who had been "instrumental in reopening the copper mine," to run for supervisor of Odell Township.

By about 11:00 all the customers were gone from the diner and I went up to the counter and talked to Trish quietly so that Jane couldn't hear from the booth. Aside from telling Trish about the proof I hoped to present to Ollie Rasmusson, I don't remember exactly what I told her, but I do remember the feeling that I had when I reached over the counter to kiss her. I felt like this could be good-bye if I were caught breaking into the church.

"I'll call you by Sunday night," I told Trish, just as my parents arrived at the diner to retrieve Jane and me.

"What's the matter?" my sister asked me as we left.

"Nothing," I said, trying to smile. "Why'd you ask?" I couldn't fool my little sister, though. Jane stared at me in a questioning way all the way home.

My nervousness kept growing Friday night and Saturday. I could hear my heart pounding continually, like a drumbeat that got faster and faster. On Saturday Jane and I watched cartoons and then the "Creature Features" movie hosted by Ollie Rasmusson. Later in the afternoon, Mom decided that we should make a "Monahan stew." As I worked on it with my family in the kitchen, I started feeling sentimental. At the counter was Dad, a serious look on his face as he cut the meat into little cubes. At the sink was Mom, looking dreamily out at the pine trees while she washed off the vegetables. Next to me at the table was my dear little sister, who was helping me cut up the carrots, celery, and onions. I realized that if something went wrong, this could be the last night I'd ever be with them. When Jane stared up at me, I said, "Boy, these onions make your eyes water!" and wiped my eyes. Then I blurted out, "I always liked making stews together like this!"

"Why, so do I, son," said Dad, but Mom looked at me in surprise and Jane continued to stare at me suspiciously.

After dinner I decided that I'd better give myself some kind of protection in case I was caught. I wrote out a letter to Mom and Dad stating everything I knew about the Copper Creekers and explaining what I'd be doing Sunday. After I finished the note, I took one of Mom's envelopes and placed it inside. I was just sealing the note when Jane came into my room without knocking.

"What's the matter, Big Butt?" my sister asked, still glaring at me suspiciously.

"Nothing. Why'd you ask?"

"You look white and your hand's shaking, and I came into your room without knocking and called you Big Butt and you didn't call me a moron."

"Jane," I said, pulling her to me by the elbow. "Can you do the biggest favor of your life for me without asking any questions about it?" She looked scared, but nodded. She agreed to tell Mom and Dad I'd gone over to see Trish on Sunday morning, and to give them the note if I didn't return home by 3:00 in the afternoon. "You *promise* you won't read that note or show it to them before three o'clock tomorrow afternoon?" I repeated. My sister seemed a little insulted at that. "I said I'd do it," she told me.

About an hour later I said good-night to the three of them, set my digital, and tried to go to sleep. I kept falling asleep and having the same dream again and again. I was in the church basement and suddenly the aliens were all around me with their faces smiling and knives in their hands. Just as they started to walk toward me, I would wake up.

I was lying there after awakening for about the third time from that nightmare when I heard some low thunder rolls off in the distance. A couple minutes later I could hear the wind swishing through the trees, and rain began pelting the roof. The thunder claps came steadily closer, as if they were marching my way, and finally they were so loud they made the walls of our cottage tremble. A few minutes later the storm passed over, and gradually the time between the flashes and the booms became greater. The rain had let up until it was just a patter on the roof and the wind had turned to a sweet-smelling wet breeze by the time my digital said 4:00 A.M.

I must have snoozed a bit because I was startled when the alarm beeped at 5:00. I immediately sat up in bed, moved the curtain away from my window, and looked outside. There was just a light rain falling from the purple-gray dawn sky.

Once I was dressed, I crept as quietly as I could into the living room and out the front door. I found the backpack where I'd left it, behind the office counter. I slung it over my shoulders and then hopped onto the Schwinn to begin the two-mile ride to downtown Copper Creek.

14

The Weird Room

By the time I reached Highway 2, the drizzle had stopped and pinkish clouds were floating quickly across the light blue sky. There were no cars on the highway at that early hour, so I was able to make the two-mile ride in just a few minutes. When the DOWNTOWN COPPER CREEK sign came into view, I got off the Schwinn and made a squiggly line in the gravel alongside the highway to mark the spot. I walked the bike into the woods and left it lying between a couple bushes, then walked the quarter mile or so through the woods to the big church.

A large field had been cleared in back of the church. In the middle of the field was a bandstand with a banner across it saying WELCOME TO THE 1ST ANNUAL COPPER CREEK PICNIC, and scattered about the field were a Ferris wheel, a merry-go-round, several other rides, and a few ticket booths and trailers.

The forest led almost up to the side of the church, so that's where I decided to break in. I hid behind a big hemlock tree and stared at the side windows for several minutes.

When I was satisfied that there was no sign of activity inside the dark church, I dashed up to one of the side windows and then crouched down against the wall while taking a long screwdriver from my backpack. Then I stood up, placed the tool in the crack beneath the window, and pried. The window went up just a bit. I squeezed my fingertips under the window and lifted until my fingers turned bone white. Suddenly there was a cracking sound and the window went up.

I climbed in through the window as quickly as I could and closed it behind me. It was dark in the room, but I didn't want to turn on the light for fear of attracting attention. As I waited for my eyes to adjust to the darkness, I realized that I could still feel the thud-thud-thud of my heartbeat but that somehow I was less nervous doing this than I had been thinking about it. When my eyes cleared, I saw that I was in a room with a green chalkboard, a large table and chairs, and a bookcase containing about two dozen identical Bibles.

Elsewhere on the main floor I found two other Sunday School rooms, a kitchen, several offices and bathrooms, and a large auditorium. When I was convinced that no one else was in the church, I went down the stairs into a short corridor. I found only two rooms down there. One was an open storage room filled with chairs and tables. The other had to be the mysterious room Uncle Myron had glimpsed, but the big metal door leading to it was locked.

I looked around in the storage room for a while to see if there was some way to get from there into the locked room. By the time I gave up on that idea it was about 6:30, meaning that I probably had at most two hours before the aliens arrived for Sunday church services. I went upstairs and spent a few minutes searching through Reverend Smith's office for papers or anything else that would prove what they were, but there were just a few papers in his desk and none of them proved anything.

I was beginning to think that I would have to hide in there and tape-record their conversations to prove anything when it occurred to me that perhaps there was a way to get into the locked room from upstairs. I explored the main floor rooms again, and on the auditorium wall behind the pulpit I found a large rectangular grating covering the heating duct. Peering inside, I saw that it was large enough for me to climb through.

I figured that the duct probably led downstairs to the furnace, and that since I'd seen no furnace in the storage room, it had to be in the locked room. I went down to get a long rope I'd seen tied around some chairs in the storage room. Back upstairs I used my screwdriver and pliers to get the grating off the duct. After tying one end of the rope around the leg of the organ, I removed my backpack and crawled headfirst into the duct, releasing the rope from my hand as I went.

The duct went sideways for several yards and then curved downward. I went down a few feet and then came to an elbow-shaped piece of piping that led down into the furnace. I held my breath as I placed my hand against the elbow-shaped piece of piping. It moved when I shoved hard against it. The blood was rushing to my head as I hung there like a bat, and I was also getting pretty exhausted, so I

137

backed myself up to the auditorium and sat there for a while. When I felt better, I took the screwdriver out of the backpack and crawled back down through the duct. I pushed and shoved and pried, and finally the elbow-shaped piece crashed down to the floor beneath me. Through the opening I'd made in the duct, I could see the floor of the locked room just a few feet below.

I went back up to the auditorium and sat until my head cleared, and then I went back down the duct feetfirst. When I reached the opening I'd made in the duct, I placed my feet through and lowered myself gradually downward. I ran out of rope a little way off the floor, but it was no problem jumping the last couple feet.

When I looked around the room, I was disappointed at first. It seemed to be just a huge warehouse. There was a section for pots and pans, one for beds, one for bicycles, another for lawn chairs, another for appliances, and so on. There was little variety within each section. In the furniture section there were only two kinds of sofas, and in the book section there were maybe twenty different books with about a hundred copies of each. The main way things varied was by color—for example, there were blue, red, and yellow bicycles.

Before beginning my search for concrete proof, I had to take care of some things upstairs. I unlocked the big metal door and climbed the stairs to the main floor, where I retrieved the backpack and rope and screwed the grating in the auditorium back into place. I lugged the ladder I'd seen in the storage room into the warehouse, used it to put the elbow-shaped piece of piping back into place, then lugged it back to the storage room. Once I was satisfied that everything was back together properly, I went back to the weird room, closed the door behind me (making sure it locked again), and began my exploration.

Against one wall were five metal boxes of various sizes— the "weird machines" Uncle Myron had seen. The smallest was no larger than a toaster oven and the biggest was almost the size of a garage. Next to the machines were large bins filled with metal, plastic, glass, wood, and other assorted junk.

Leading from the machines was a kind of railroad track, which I followed all the way across the warehouse into a short tunnel. At the end of the tunnel was a garage door, which must have opened to the outside. Two large carts were sitting at the end of the track, right in front of the garage door.

Bewildered by what all this meant, I was walking through the appliance section when I saw a familiar-looking TV. It was the one that had been stolen out of Cottage One the summer before. Then I saw that there were six other TVs precisely like it in the appliance section—even with the same exact scratches!

I had gone back and was looking at the smallest machine to try to figure out how it worked when I heard sounds upstairs. Someone had entered the church. A few minutes later I heard a second person enter. Praying that I had put everything back in its exact place up there, I went into the tunnel to hide just in case someone came downstairs.

I waited until about 8:00, when people began to arrive for

the Sunday morning services. There was a murmuring of voices in the auditorium for a while, then someone began playing the organ, and shortly after that it became quiet. By the time Reverend Smith began talking to his "people," I had the tape recorder set up and recording next to the heating duct, where I could hear him pretty well.

"First point of business," I heard Reverend Smith say. "It's been reported that several of you have been talking in private about us being—shall we say—from an unusual place. Starting right after this meeting, let none of us ever again—even if just two of us are alone in a room together—talk about us being from an unusual place. Agreed?"

"Agreed," they chorused.

"Let us bow our heads in prayer," said Reverend Smith. After a brief pause for silent prayer, he continued. "Point number two. This coming week another group of our people is arriving. Work will begin soon on housing for them, but for several months we'll be having them as guests in our homes. Volunteers to house the newcomers please sign this sheet at the pulpit on the way out. By the way, where are the newcomers from?"

"Virginia," they all said.

"Correct. Point number three. We're doing fine so far—two of us engaged to marry people from Odell. But, as a man who respects the biblical command to be fruitful and multiply, let me say that we could do better. Dwayne, how are you doing with that girl, Kathy?"

"Fine, sir," answered Dwayne, after which they all laughed.

"Do you think I may be officiating at a happy occasion—say by next summer, Dwayne?"

"You mean *marry* her?" asked Dwayne. "I'm only supposed to be—I mean, I'm only eighteen."

"So what?" answered Reverend Smith. "People have been getting married at eighteen for ages. Work on it, Dwayne. If you do get married, let me suggest Ohio as a good place to settle. As the Bible says, the farther and wider we spread the word, the sooner we're all safe. My own daughter is moving to California after she marries Chief McMaster's son.

"The last point. I've heard that one of us has been telling people that we should read and improve our minds. Do I need to remind you of the trouble thinking caused on our planet? We need to work toward a nice, peaceful way of life with good food, fun, and other pleasant things. We must work to stamp out thinking here, just as we did at home. Agreed?"

"Agreed!" they echoed. But then I heard the unmistakable voice of Marsha Coe say, "I don't agree. I've been to the library. I've seen what lovely things they've written, their beautiful paintings, their philosophy and great achievements. I think we could try to improve our minds and still fit in with them—"

"Don't call them *them!*" Reverend Smith said. "But since you brought it up, Miss Coe, let me talk plainly. We know that thanks to thinking we almost blew ourselves out of the Galaxy several times. Marsha, don't you realize that we're going to be their saviors, not their conquerors? More of us

141

will land, and we'll spread out among them, and in a couple generations they—*we*—will be like the nice pleasant folks you see on TV, with of course a wild boy, bad guy, or loose woman here and there just for a little variety. We're really taking the best idea they've created and making it real."

"We don't have the right to do it to them!" Marsha said.

"It's not a matter of *rights!*" answered Reverend Smith. "We're doing it because we have to blend in and make room for our people to live—and it's what they like anyway. Marsha, we've been pretty easy on you considering that at least two of them found out about us thanks to you. And I should tell you that people have already advised me to take drastic action about this thinking business of yours. I only hope it won't be needed.

"On a happier note, let's hope you young folks use the picnic to mingle. Who knows? Today's picnic could lead to a couple more marriages. Let us bow our heads in prayer. Amen."

After they began leaving the church, I turned off the tape recorder and went into the tunnel to wait until they were all gone. I was about to leave the tunnel and go back to investigating the strange machines when I heard someone coming down the stairs. I went to the edge of the tunnel, and from my hiding place there I heard a key turn in the big metal door, and then saw Mr. and Mrs. Davis enter the weird room.

Mr. Davis took a dollar bill out of his wallet and placed it inside the smallest duplicating machine while his wife put in paper. As the machine began to hum, Mr. Davis said, "Press the dealie to get all the numbers different."

142

A few seconds later there was a *PING*, and as Mr. Davis removed stacks of money from the little machine everything became clear. The metal boxes were like Xerox machines, only instead of making copies of just paper they could make copies of things like TVs or money or whatever the aliens needed! I took a picture of Mr. Davis taking some of the money out of the machine. My heart began to pound in excitement, because I figured that as soon as Mr. and Mrs. Davis were gone, I could grab the smallest duplicating machine and carry it out of there for the proof I needed.

After Mr. and Mrs. Davis left, I waited a couple minutes until I was sure it was quiet upstairs. I came out of my hiding place and was about to pick up the little duplicating machine when I heard more sounds upstairs. I was back inside the tunnel by the time Dwayne Coe and Bob Davis entered the room.

"It's a royal pain having to do this today," Dwayne complained to Bob.

"Well, I guess someone's got to do the work today," Bob Davis answered, in that all-American-boy way of his.

"Yeah, but why us? Well, we might as well get started. Got the list?"

Pulling a piece of paper out of his hip pocket, Bob said, "Let's do your dad's stuff first."

I watched as Dwayne and Bob took two TVs off the shelf and put them inside two medium-sized duplicating machines. Dwayne and Bob then shovelled glass, metal, plastic, and other things from the bins into a section of each box. After that they closed the doors of the machines and pressed a button on each. Lights flashed from inside the machines, and there were crunching and clanging sounds and a loud hum. I watched them make about fifty TV sets and just as many radios, and I got a few decent pictures of them doing it. When they were done with the radios, Dwayne looked at the list and said, "Now we need to make some clothes for the newcomers."

Dwayne went and got several garments from the clothes section. He and Bob shovelled a bunch of what looked like cotton into three of the machines. Then Dwayne placed a sweater in one of the machines and a light jacket in the second. The third garment was a pair of ladies' underpants. "Hey, look at this, Bob," Dwayne said, holding up the underpants. Dwayne gave a moronic laugh as he placed the underpants in the machine.

As the three machines flashed, clanged, and hummed, Dwayne suddenly snapped his fingers and said, "Oh JEEZ, we forgot to hit the color thingamajigs. I'll get this one," he said, tapping a couple buttons. Bob hurriedly pushed buttons on the two other machines. A couple minutes later there were three loud *PINGS*.

As they started to take the clothes out of the machines, Bob said, "Should we put all this junk in the carts over there?" and pointed to the tunnel where I was hiding. I reached into my backpack and pulled out a hammer in case I had to defend myself, but luckily Dwayne said, "Naaa, let's just leave this junk on the shelves and let someone else get it ready to distribute later." Then they piled up the radios and TVs in the appliance section and placed the

144

different-colored jackets, sweaters, and underpants in the clothes section.

"Hey, Bob," Dwayne said, "before we do all the laundry detergents, let's go over to my place and get a couple brewskis. Dad's got a bunch in the fridge."

"I don't know, Dwayne, we're three years below the legal drinking age. Anyway, if we want beers we can put some barley and stuff in the machine and make them."

"They come out tasting generic, I've tried it," said Dwayne. "Come on, don't be a wimp. Dad'll never miss them."

I waited several minutes until they were out of the building, and then I went over to the wall with the five duplicating machines against it. The smallest one was no heavier than a toaster oven. Just for an extra piece of proof, I took a dollar bill out of my wallet, placed some paper in the little machine as I'd seen Mrs. Davis do, and pressed the buttons until I got it to start. A few seconds later I had a stack of identical one-dollar bills, which I placed in my backpack.

I then picked up the little duplicating machine, carried it to the door, and walked as quietly as I could up the stairs with it. When I reached the top of the stairs, I looked around to make sure that there were no signs of activity on the main floor. I was so excited to be leaving the church with the proof I wanted that as I headed for the Sunday School room where I'd climbed in through the window, my hands and legs were trembling.

I was about to enter the Sunday School room when suddenly the front door of the church burst open.

"You could use a few bucks, too, couldn't—" Dwayne was saying to Bob Davis as they walked in. I dashed to the Sunday School room, but Bob and Dwayne had thrown down their beers and were right behind me. There was no time to open the window, so I hurled the little duplicating machine as hard as I could at the window and exploded the glass. I pushed away a jagged piece of glass with my hand and was just about to dive out the window when a big hand on my neck yanked me back inside. When Dwayne pulled me like that, my shoulder was slammed down against the remaining glass on the window and I felt something sharp pierce my skin.

"Bob, look what this little turkey was doing!" Dwayne said, twisting me hard by the neck until I was standing very close to him. "He was stealin' one of our doohickeys. Why'd ya do that, creep?" Dwayne asked, and then slammed me down hard to the floor. "Lucky we came when we did, Bob, or he'd have gotten away with that thing. Bob, bring the doohickey back inside and then go get Reverend Smith. I'll take him downstairs."

"I don't know what's going to happen to you," Bob Davis said, as Dwayne yanked me to my feet. "Here we are trying to make a nice, pleasant world, and we have to turn nasty just because of you and your uncle. I'd sure hate to be in your shoes, Shelley."

Bob Davis went out the front door, and then Dwayne pushed and shoved me down the stairs and back into the weird room. There was something red on my jacket—blood from when my shoulder had been slammed down against

146

the broken glass on the window. Once we were back downstairs, Dwayne shoved me down to the floor again and said, "I hope you don't think I like pushin' you around. I'd much rather be home watching TV!" I was lying there reaching for the hammer in my backpack when Bob returned with Reverend Smith.

The minister stared at me with his watery gray eyes for a short while, and then as I stood up, he said, "When Mr. Hopkins over at the hospital said you wanted to have something analyzed, I knew it was time to get rid of you just as we did your uncle. It just goes to show, Dwayne, that when you go against what you know is right, you're always the loser."

"Don't talk about 'right,'" I said. "You don't know what that—" Dwayne slugged me in the stomach, and as I lay there trying to catch my breath, he said, "Shut up!"

"Dwayne, there's no need for such brutality—here, take this," Reverend Smith said, pulling a revolver from his suit coat pocket and handling it to Dwayne. "It's just a darn shame we couldn't have gone on being nice, pleasant people," Reverend Smith told me. "We would have, but you and your uncle made it necessary for us to develop a nasty streak. Well," he sighed, "in order to make a pleasant world, sometimes you have to have a bit of unpleasantness. Now I've got to think of what to do with you. We certainly can't shoot him," Reverend Smith said to Dwayne and Bob, "because somebody might get suspicious."

"There's still some of Dad's poison left," Bob Davis offered, eagerly hoping for approval.

"Nice thinking, son," Reverend Smith said, "but it's not

147

so good to use the same thing twice in a row."

"He could fall in the creek and drown like they had on 'Magnum' the other day," Dwayne Coe suggested, as he pointed the gun at me.

"Not a bad idea," said the minister. "But I was thinking more in the line of—" He moved closer to Dwayne and Bob and whispered something to them. Then, handing Dwayne his keys, Reverend Smith said aloud, "The picnic will be starting soon, boys, so I'd better get out there. You two take him out through the tunnel exit, okay?"

Once Reverend Smith had left, Dwayne and Bob started to walk me toward the tunnel. "I'm really scared, Dwayne. I've never killed anyone before," Bob said, and Dwayne told him, "Don't be a wimp." As terrified as I felt, my brain was still working at full speed and I felt a tremendous surge of energy. I knew that my best chance was to walk with Dwayne and Bob into the tunnel and then try to break away from them in the darkness and head for the stairs. We were about to enter the tunnel when a key turned in the big metal door to the basement, and in walked Marsha Coe.

"What are you doin' here?" Dwayne asked his sister.

Marsha took one look at me, another at her brother holding the gun, and then walked quickly toward us. "What are *you* doing here?" she asked her brother.

"What does it look like?" Dwayne said in disgust. "You were wrong about this turkey being harmless, Sis. We caught him trying to steal one of our gizmos," he said, pointing to the duplicating machines near the wall. "We're just followin' Reverend Smith's orders."

148

"And just what—" Marsha began, but then suddenly she dove at her brother's arm and pushed it so that the gun was no longer aimed at me. "*Run*, Shelley!" she screamed. I ran straight for the big metal door as fast as I could, but when I reached it I glanced back for an instant. Dwayne had shoved Marsha down and was aiming the gun straight at me. The last thing I saw before I went out the door was Marsha hurling herself in front of Dwayne's line of fire. The next second a shot rang out and I was heading up the stairs.

I went into the Sunday School room where I'd broken in and crawled headfirst through the empty window frame. After landing on the ground, I picked myself up and headed into the woods. I was afraid they'd catch me if I rode my bike on the highway, so I ran through the trees beside the road. On and on I ran, until my legs felt so weak that I couldn't even feel the ground beneath me, until my head was swimming crazily and I was gasping for air. After what must have been a couple miles, I realized that they weren't chasing me, and I fell down in complete exhaustion behind a tree and lay for a while listening to the pounding of my heart.

When I had regained some of my energy, I stood up. I had lost my sense of direction in the woods, and I didn't know which was the way to Odell. I stood there for a while until I heard a car passing on the highway. From that, I recalculated my directions and began walking to Odell. Staying in the woods as far as possible, I reached the pretty little town by about 11:30.

15

We Humans Strike Back

When I got to Odell I walked up Iron Street, past the locked-up diner and the theater. I turned the corner, walked by the library, and found the building that had a sign on its roof saying WKRL—ODELL. As I opened the front door, I took one last glimpse down the street. No one had followed me.

Inside the building, a gray-haired receptionist was sitting at the front desk watching a small TV.

"Hi," I said to her. "I'd like to see Mr. Rasmusson. He knows I might be coming."

The woman stared at the bloodstain on the shoulder of my jacket and then nodded toward a chair. After I sat down, she picked up the phone and talked to someone. A few seconds later a middle-aged guy wearing a suit jacket and tie on top and blue jeans and cowboy boots on his lower half came hurrying down a corridor. He had the same pink face, millions of black curls, and boyish smile as Ollie Rasmusson, but for a second I wasn't sure it was Ollie because he looked so much older than he did on TV and seemed to be much more in a hurry. Before he greeted me, he said, "Just a second," and looked through the memos sitting on the desk next to the phone. Then he came up to me and asked, "You're Shelley?"

Ollie led me down the corridor and into a small conference room. After we'd sat down, he looked at my blood-stained shoulder and asked, "What happened to you?"

I told him the whole story about the aliens, ending with my escape from the church basement. "Mr. Rasmusson, if you run a story saying we know what the aliens are, they'll see it on TV and leave," I explained. "You also may be saving my life, because I'm the biggest threat they have."

Ollie glanced toward the corridor uncertainly and then said, "Let me have the film." After removing the roll from the camera, he picked up the phone and spoke. A short while later, a young woman he called Margo came to take the film away. Looking at his watch, Ollie said, "I've got to go do the newsbreak. Come on."

He led me into a control room, inside which a man was sitting on a tall stool and watching the old movie that was being shown on a monitor. "Al's director, cameraman, and a lot of other things around here," Ollie explained to me. "Al, let Shelley watch in here. But be quiet, Shelley," Ollie said. Through the large glass window of the control room, I watched Ollie walk out into the studio and sit down at the desk where he always delivered the news. Just a few feet from the desk was the creepy-looking cardboard castle that formed the "Creature Features" background, and not far from that was the goofy-looking cardboard castle that was the "Ollie's Place" background.

At about five minutes to twelve Margo, the young woman who had taken my film, came into the studio. She helped Ollie put on some makeup and then began fiddling with the camera. Ollie studied the papers on his desk for a few more minutes. At noon the red light on the camera went on, and when I looked up at the monitor, there was Ollie wearing the suit top and tie and seriously beginning the news, just as I'd seen him do many times before:

> Good afternoon. Our top story today is a local one. WKRL news has just learned that a teenaged Copper Creek girl was shot and wounded shortly after ten o'clock this morning. Thirteen-year-old Marsha Coe suffered a bullet wound to the abdomen and is in critical condition in Odell's Grand View Hospital. Early reports indicate that Miss Coe was shot while surprising vandals who had broken into the Copper Creek Universal Humanist Church. The Copper Creek picnic has been postponed due to the incident . . .

I had seen Marsha dive in front of Dwayne's gun and had heard the shot, but until Ollie Rasmusson told the story on the news I had somehow hoped that Marsha hadn't really been hurt. Preventing her brother from shooting me might cost Marsha her life, I realized. I knew I had to think up ways to convince Ollie to do a report on the aliens, but I found it hard to think of anything except Marsha's hurling herself in front of that gun for my sake.

When Ollie finished the news, he returned to the control room and led me back to the conference room we'd been in before. "Can I listen to the tape you said you got?" he asked me. I took out Mom's tape player, rewound the tape, and played Reverend Smith's sermon. The problem was that it was pretty garbled and you could barely make out what Reverend Smith was saying. Ollie played portions of it several times and then shook his head.

"Let me explain something, Shelley," he began, but was interrupted by the young women returning with the photographs I'd taken.

"Ollie, you and Al have an appointment at two o'clock to interview the doctor who took out the bullet and the girl's family over at Grand View. I'm going out now to get some shots of the church and interview the minister."

After she left, Ollie and I looked at the photograph of Mr. Davis taking the stack of money out of the machine and the pictures of Dwayne Coe and Bob Davis taking TVs and radios out. Shaking his head again, Ollie said, "You can't tell what those machines are, and you can't see what they're doing too well. Let me explain something to you, Shelley. There's nothing I'd love more than to have this story be true, because if I were the first to report a true story about aliens I could get away from this dinky place and get a job at the network. But—see, I'm not saying I don't believe you, but you need a lot of proof for something like this. You know what I'd look like if I went on TV and said the Copper Creekers were really murdering lizards from space and that wasn't true? I'd be the laughing stock of the electronic broadcasting industry, I'd have my pants sued off, I'd be used as an example in *textbooks* of a guy who didn't check out his stories, I'd be—"

"But what if the story's true and you don't report it?" I asked him. "You'd be used as an example of a guy who passed up the greatest story of all time."

"I'm not going to pass it up," he answered. "I'm just going to do more checking when I have time. This just isn't proof, Shelley," he said, holding up the blurry photo of Mr. Davis taking the stack of what I knew was money out of the machine. "I'll see that you get a ride home if you're—"

The photograph suddenly reminded me of something. "Wait a second," I interrupted, unzipping my backpack. I took the stack of dollar bills I'd made out of my backpack and said, "Look at the serial numbers."

As Ollie shuffled through the money and compared the serial numbers, there was a growing look of amazement on his face. "They're all the same!" he said.

"Yeah, and the same as this one," I said, taking the dollar bill that I'd used to make them out of my wallet. "And you know why?" I continued, handing it to him. "Because I made it on the machine I was telling you about. I forgot I'd done that."

Looking up from the bills, Ollie said, "There's no doubt that these are counterfeit. There's something we can do with this. I've got to work on the story about the girl who got shot, but if you can wait here, we'll work up a story when I get back."

When Ollie started to get up, I was so disgusted that I no longer cared what I said to him. "You're just going to go to the hospital and see her bleeding real blood, and you're going to come back here doubting me again," I said, zipping the money back up in my backpack. "Well, forget it, Mr. Rasmusson, there's plenty of other TV stations I can go to. I'll hitchhike to the one in Duluth, or I'll call the network. You either decide to do a story on it right now, or forget it. I want you to put the story in as a bulletin—and I want it in by two o'clock."

Ollie stared at me with a little smile, but when he saw that I was keeping a stone face, it disappeared. "But I've got to get a release from your parents if—"

"If that's your decision, so long," I said, figuring I would call my parents from Trish's apartment and then try to get them to take me to the TV station in Duluth.

"Wait a second, hold it a second," he said. I stood over him as he placed his face down in his hands. When he picked it up he looked nervous. "Okay," he said. "I'm either going to be very famous in an hour, or—I don't even want to think about it," he said, pushing away from the table with his hand.

We went back out to Ollie's desk in the studio, where he had me go through the story once more, all the while taking notes on it. He then spent a half hour writing out his story while asking me more questions.

When Ollie finished writing out his story, he motioned to Al to come out into the studio. Ollie had me wait in the control room while he spoke to Al, who had a look of disbelief on his face and kept shaking his head no. Ollie talked to him some more, and finally Al shrugged. A few minutes later Margo returned and joined the conversation.

At ten to two, Ollie sat down at his desk and motioned me to come out there. As I sat down next to Ollie, Margo took her position behind the camera and Al returned to the control room.

"We're going to wing it live," Ollie told me. "Take out that money and hold it up to the camera when I tell you to. Don't be nervous, just answer the questions I ask you and look sincere."

Sitting in the chair next to Ollie, I could see the monitor on the far wall. A movie I knew was being shown—*The Beast with a Million Eyes.* Suddenly in the middle of an exciting scene, the image of the beast disappeared, and there was a close-up of Ollie Rasmusson sitting at his desk. The next second he was saying:

> We interrupt this program for a special news bulletin. WKRL news has just obtained exclusive information that a counterfeiting ring is operating out of the nearby town of Copper Creek, Michigan. Here are some of the fake bills obtained from the basement of the Copper Creek Universal Humanist Church.

As I held up the bills, I could see on the monitor that the camera had zoomed in to take a close-up of them. Then Ollie continued:

> There is a bizarre aspect to this story that has not been verified as yet. There are indications that the beings who made these bills are actually aliens from another planet. For that aspect of the story we turn to fourteen-year-old Shelley Monahan, who obtained these bills in the basement of the Copper Creek Universal Humanist Church. Tell us how you obtained these bills, Shelley.

156

"Well," I began, "it all started when my Uncle Myron and I saw this flying saucer go right over our heads last summer . . . " It must have been the longest news bulletin in history, because for the next ten minutes everything that had happened with the aliens gushed right out of me.

When I finished and the movie came back on, the phones started ringing all over the place in there.

Ollie picked his phone off his desk, listened for a while, and then said, "But—but—" and placed it back on the hook. "The owner of the station," he told me. "I think I've got about a ninety-nine percent chance of being fired." His phone kept ringing, but Ollie didn't answer it because he was sitting with his head in his hands saying, "It wasn't such a bad job here," over and over to himself.

Finally the gray-haired receptionist came back to the studio and told Ollie, "It's Chief McMaster. He wants to talk to you."

"Great. Now I'm going to be arrested. Yel-lo," he said, forlornly. Ollie listened for a while and then said, "No, sir, I wasn't drinking . . . . I did it because I believed him . . . . I know your son's going to marry one of them . . . . Yes, if I'm wrong I'll be glad to do a retraction."

For the next few minutes Al and Margo continued to answer the phone and say they knew nothing about it, but Ollie and I just sat there without saying a word to each other while his phone rang. Sitting there like that, I began feeling sick to my stomach. My uncle was dead, my girl friend had nearly been run over, a couple hours earlier the aliens had tried to kill me, I was sitting in this forlorn little studio with

Ollie, and now, after all that, it looked like the TV bulletin wouldn't do any good. I had really believed that the aliens would just disappear once their identity was revealed on TV.

The calls were starting to taper off when the gray-haired receptionist returned and said, "It's Chief McMaster again, Ollie."

"He's going to lock me up right *now!*" Ollie said, taking the phone. "Yel-lo," he said into it. As he listened, I saw his lower jaw slowly drop. After hanging up the phone Ollie said, "I'll be switched!" almost in a whisper, and then stared out into space.

"What happened?" I asked him. When Ollie continued to just stare at the wall I shook him by the shoulders and repeated, "What happened, Ollie?"

"Three flying saucers just left Copper Creek!" he said. "Hundreds of people saw it," Ollie added. "Do you know what this means? Do you realize what a monumental event this is? Thank you, Shelley!" He was getting so happy and excited I thought he was going to cry, but I felt so drained all I could do was shake his hand and say, "Thanks, Ollie."

I dragged myself out of the station and went around the corner to the Vincents' apartment. They had the TV on, and I could see Ollie Rasmusson giving a report on how the flying saucers had just been spotted leaving Copper Creek.

As her father and Aunt Theresa watched Ollie's report, Trish kept giving me little kisses and saying, "You *did* it, you got rid of them!" When the report ended, Mr. Vincent and Aunt Theresa congratulated me and began asking me all kinds of questions about the aliens.

158

After answering a few of them I excused myself, went to the phone, and called the Grand View Hospital. The nurse there told me that Marsha had been carried away by her family right after the bulletin had been given on TV. "In her condition, I doubt that she could survive," the nurse said. I had managed to keep a stone face while my life had been in danger, but somehow I burst into tears when I heard that about Marsha. After pulling myself together, I phoned Mom and asked her and Dad to come get me.

* * *

During the next few days I became a celebrity. Newspapers took my picture and interviewed me. *Time, Newsweek, People, The National Enquirer,* and about ten other magazines did stories, too. I was interviewed on a couple national TV shows, and I even got a call from the president of the United States. But when the network that hired Ollie wanted me to help on a made-for-TV movie, I wouldn't have anything to do with it. I remembered just how impossible it had been to convince anyone of the truth, and the idea of making money off what had happened to Uncle Myron and Marsha made me sick.

Despite the hubbub, I had a pretty good time during our last few weeks at the resort. My family and the Vincents and Aunt Theresa and Harv and Betty Holmquist had a quiet little party to honor what I had done with my Uncle Myron's help. Being told I'd done something great by those people meant a lot more to me than having a TV interviewer say it right after doing a dog food commercial. Trish and I also played fast-pitch and went to movies, and on the last night of my family's vacation she and I observed the Perseid meteor shower together.

When we got back to Chicago in the middle of August, it was nice being home and getting treated like the greatest hero of all time by my friends and relatives, but I missed Trish a lot. As I write this, it's the day before Thanksgiving, 1985, and Trish and her dad have moved back to Detroit. I don't think I'll be seeing them when we go back to Copper Creek next summer to the resort that Uncle Myron left us in his will, but Detroit's not so far from home, and I know I'll see her again.

There're a couple things that'll always bother me about the whole experience. I'm not really sure we drove out all the aliens. As I walk along Roscoe Street or any other street, I see strings of living rooms with TVs flickering inside. At school I hear kids talking about the programs they watch, and even when I overhear strangers talking, it's often about a TV show. I've also noticed that there are a lot of people who like to talk and act like characters on TV. Sometimes I think that the aliens have been among us for many years, or that they've just moved to other places, or that more have come.

One other thing. I'm crazy about Trish—you know that. But sometimes I look up at the stars and think about the girl who saved my life—that beautiful, golden-haired Marsha Coe.